It was her wedding day

In mere hours she would marry Jake Merit, the man of her dreams. Susan stretched and started to sit up, then sank back to stare at the ceiling. This should be the happiest day of her life.

"I love you, Jake," she murmured, wishing their relationship was such that she could say it to him. They hadn't even kissed. Of course, that was entirely her fault. He'd tried to kiss her to seal their engagement, but at the last second she'd panicked and turned away, unable to bear his mercy kisses.

She would have to change her tune about that, and fast. Mercy kisses or no, she'd pledged herself to him, and that meant accepting whatever crumbs of affection he offered her. Within hours she would be his wife, and she had promised him children....

Dear Reader,

I had so much fun with my ENCHANTED BRIDES trilogy, I decided it would be exciting to write a series about three brothers. I envisaged each brother to be tough and successful in his own right, but lonely—whether he realizes it or not. Then I decided to place these men on a mountain of emeralds located on their own private island.

The heirs to the Merit emerald dynasty—Jake, Marc and Zack—are as different as brothers can be. But what they have in common is that they are all gorgeous men—who are each about to meet the one special woman for them.

I hope you enjoy Jake's story, Honeymoon Hitch. He learns about himself, about life and especially about love when Susan O'Conner steps onto his island, knocks him off balance and ultimately wins his stubborn heart.

All my best,

Renee Roszel

P.S. I love to hear from readers, so do, please, write to me at P.O. Box 700154, Tulsa, Oklahoma 74107.

THE MERITS OF MARRIAGE

The Merit brothers—it takes three special women to win their stubborn hearts

Look for Marc's story in
Coming Home To Wed
Harlequin Romance #3603, May 2000
from Renee Roszel

Honeymoon Hitch

Renee Roszel

THE MERITS OF MARRIAGE

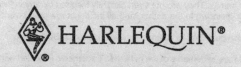

HARLEQUIN®

TORONTO • NEW YORK • LONDON
AMSTERDAM • PARIS • SYDNEY • HAMBURG
STOCKHOLM • ATHENS • TOKYO • MILAN • MADRID
PRAGUE • WARSAW • BUDAPEST • AUCKLAND

To Dick Harnett
Thanks for the emeralds
and the muffins

ISBN 0-373-03599-3

HONEYMOON HITCH

First North American Publication 2000.

Visit us at www.romance.net

Printed in U.S.A.

CHAPTER ONE

"MR. MERIT is expecting you, miss." The servant laid a hand on the ornate silver doorknob and bowed slightly.

Susan swallowed, tried to speak, but ended up able to do no more than nod. *Get a grip, Susan,* she warned silently. *Since when has the prospect of facing a man made you quiver like a rabbit? All little-girl fantasies have to come to an end. Today is simply the day Jake Merit's pedestal topples.*

It had been thirteen years since she'd seen him. She'd been a very impressionable fifteen-year-old, all giggly over her first big crush. No flesh-and-bone man could measure up to the image she'd constructed of Jake Merit. If the shrine her fantasies had built to his perfection had been created from brick and mortar, it would rival the Great Wall of China, and be visible from the moon.

She heard a rattle, and realized the butler was opening one of the massive oak doors. Without a whisper of sound he slipped past her, blocking her view of the room. "Mr. Merit, Miss O'Conner."

Susan blinked, which was all the time it took for the butler to slip back out and disappear, leaving her standing in the hallway like a potted geranium. She stared. His office must have been huge. From her vantage point just outside she couldn't see Jake or his desk. Just a tall picture window, and way off in the distance, the Atlantic Ocean, undulating peacefully, oblivious to her turmoil.

"Miss O'Conner?" came a deep voice. "Are you out there?"

She jumped, then got herself under control. "Yes, Mr. Merit." *Don't get upset if he doesn't remember you!* she counseled. *You're here on business! You are not the schoolgirl who entertained your sister's date while he cooled his heels in the parlor. The few times you played hostess were barely an hour out of his life! Why should he remember you?*

With a hurried adjustment of her posture, Susan stepped into the room. After all, Jake Merit was only a man *"Oh!"*

She bit her tongue. Had she actually said *oh?* She knew she must have, because Jake glanced up from whatever he'd been writing, his brow knit.

He laid aside his golden pen. "Is something wrong, Miss O'Conner?"

She shook her head, berating herself for her outburst. Okay, maybe the years hadn't dimmed his good looks. Maybe she couldn't congratulate herself for building a shrine to him that was all out of proportion to reality. The man was definitely shrine-worthy. Even after all these years, his eyes were every bit as mesmerizing as she remembered—dazzling green fire, like gem quality emeralds.

She lifted her chin. "Yes—" As soon as the word was out of her mouth she realized it was the wrong answer, so she shook her head. "I mean, *no.* I just, uh, remembered I—forgot my blow-dryer." She cringed at the flimsy excuse. It wasn't even true!

"I imagine we can find a substitute." He flashed a crooked grin and pushed up to stand. She followed his rise. He was also every bit as tall as he'd been in her fantasy. And his lazy grin was every bit as titillating. Unfortunately, with an additional thirteen years of life experience under her belt, Susan wasn't pleased with the added sexual pull his grin had acquired.

She felt a little queasy, deciding she wasn't such a world-class fantasy builder, after all. If Jake wasn't every inch as devastating as she'd fantasized all these years, she'd *eat* her blow-dryer. At least, then she'd really *need* one.

He rounded his desk with an easy grace and she found it impossible to drag her attention away. He was a good-looking hunk of male animal in a white polo shirt and stone-washed jeans. She was surprised by the jeans, and even more surprised at how he managed to carry off such suave elegance dressed so casually. She'd seen lots of men in formal attire who didn't look half as princely.

Somewhere in the back of her mind, it occurred to her that Jake was walking toward her.

Toward her!

Every nerve in her body leaped and shuddered.

Jake came to a halt just outside her personal space. "So you're the competent Miss O'Conner Ed's been bragging about for the past year." His amazing eyes locked with hers. A tingle started at her nape, then danced along her nerves to every extremity of her body. "Ed tells me your presentation at the Eastern S.E.P.M. on Maine Pegmatites knocked their socks off in Providence. I understand you got the Best Paper award."

Susan was astonished that Jake knew she'd won the Society of Economic Paleontologists and Mineralogists honor. She'd been excited, naturally. Well, more like stunned, considering the competition. Her stoic boss hadn't make a big deal out of it, so she hadn't expected the word to filter up through the ranks to the CEO of their major client. "Why—thanks." She winced. How lame! Why couldn't she think of anything pithy or witty?

"It's nice to meet you." He held out a hand.

She managed to get her fingers unclenched, and inserted her hand into his. She tried not to dwell on the fact that he had no idea he'd met her before. "It's nice to meet you, too, Mr. Merit. You have lovely eyes."

His expression changed slightly, a touch of surprise widening his gaze. "Thank you. They're my mother's."

His response confused her. What was the matter? How could she lose the thread of simple, polite chatter? "Excuse me?"

"My mother's eyes were green, too."

It took a flash of a second—a horrified flash—for Susan to realize she *hadn't* said what she'd thought she said. "I…I meant…I said…you have a lovely *island!*" She prayed he'd believe that. "Not that your eyes aren't—er—I mean…your eyes are certainly nice, too."

She tugged her fingers from his grasp. Somehow, holding his hand while blurting out breathy tributes was more humiliation than she could deal with. What was the matter with her? Where was her usual self-assurance?

"I'm sorry for the misunderstanding," he said.

He didn't believe her clumsy explanation for a second. She could tell by the twinkle in his eyes. It was gracious of him to give her an easy out, since she had no desire to explain the Freudian nature of her blunder. In self-defense, she sprang to a safer subject. "I'd expected you to have a twenty-foot fence around the island, with miles of barbed wire and thirty or forty machine-gun turrets. I'm amazed at how little security there is."

His grin continued to do damage to her insides. "The best security is invisible, Miss O'Conner. You came on a Merit cruiser. Your easy access doesn't mean it's that simple for everybody."

She absorbed that. "Well, however you handle it, my

congratulations. You've managed to keep the place beautiful and apparently secure, too.''

"I'm glad you approve."

His extraordinary eyes were twinkling again. Susan knew her approval didn't mean a hill of beans to him, but she chose not to take offense even if he was being sarcastic. She'd be spending the next month on Merit Island, in charge of the annual core-hole drilling. The mineralogist who usually handled the job was Ed Sharp. He'd been assistant resource advisor for Merit Emeralds for fifteen years. Since her boss was indisposed, it became Susan's responsibility to take his place. This was a plum job, and she couldn't afford to be offended.

Besides, there was a difference between out-and-out sarcasm and harmless teasing. She remembered Jake as a nice guy. She had no intention of labeling him a superior snob or a jerk. He'd have to do a whole lot worse than tease to become a bad guy in her eyes.

He took her arm, startling her so badly, she gasped.

"Did I hurt you?" He eased his grip, though it had never been anything but gentlemanly.

She shook her head. "I didn't expect you to touch me." She wanted to bite off her tongue for that ridiculously puritanical statement.

He glanced her way, one brow slightly arched. She had the feeling he was forming an opinion about her. Probably "goosey" or "timid" or "afraid of men". None of these descriptions fit. She never gasped when a man took her arm. And she was no shrinking violet, either. Why did Jake Merit seem to be able to short-circuit her brain and make her act like a babbling idiot?

"I'll show you to your room, Miss O'Conner. I'm sure after that long trip you'd like to freshen up," he said.

"Tell me, how did Ed hurt himself, again? He was vague in his message."

Susan tried to squelch a grin. Her boss was in pain, and it wasn't funny. "His thirtieth high school reunion was last weekend," she said with as solemn an expression as she could manage. "He slipped a disk on the dance floor doing the alligator or the albatross, or something. Whatever it was, it bit him."

Jake laughed, the same throaty sound that had sent a thrill through her when he'd been a senior at Harvard. She experienced the sensation again, so strongly it seemed as if she and Jake were back in her parents' parlor, waiting for Yvette to finish primping. Susan had told the stupidest jokes, and he'd indulged her with that same mellow laugh. The sound of it still rumbled through her dreams on occasion.

As they walked, Susan hardly noticed where he led her, whether high or low, in or out. Around the edges of her consciousness, she registered that everything in the mansion radiated warmth and beauty. The wood gleamed and the crystal glistened. The place even gave off a welcoming smell. Something between freshly baked bread and Cedarwood. She inhaled, working on becoming the poised, professional woman she'd been before she'd come face-to-face with Jake again.

For all Susan knew, they might as well have been beamed up to a star, their molecules chasing around, bouncing off each other like so much space dust. She couldn't concentrate on anything but the fact that Jake smelled as inviting as his home—with a yummy dash of lemon-lime tossed in for good measure.

He stopped before a door, drawing Susan to a halt. She blinked, coming out of her haze. With a quick survey of her surroundings, she faced him, puzzled. "We're still in the mansion?"

"Of course. Where did you think you'd stay?"

"I thought—wherever Ed Sharp stayed."

Jake indicated her door. "You're there."

She absorbed this news, confused. "But—don't you have quarters for consultants?"

"We have housing for the miners. But I don't think you'd be comfortable in the barracks." He grinned. "As my mining expert, you deserve a few perks, don't you think?"

She supposed he had a point. To be honest, if it were anybody else but Jake standing beside her, she'd be thrilled to have a room in the mansion. "The barracks probably wouldn't be the best idea." She shrugged and smiled her thanks. If Ed stayed there, then she should. But the place was so huge! "I may never find my way back to your office." She felt stupid for not paying attention to where he'd led her.

Jake indicated a door across the hall. "That's my room. If I'm there, I'll escort you until you get your bearings. If I'm out, use the phone. Somebody will fetch you."

His room? Jake Merit's room was across the hall? *That's just dandy!* "Your—room?" she repeated, hoping she'd heard wrong.

"Yes." He cocked his head toward a door farther down the hall. "Adjoining my room is a den. Ed and I had late-night meetings in there." He slipped a hand into his trouser pocket. "Trust me when I say, I'll get my money's worth out of you."

She stared at his bedroom door, barely resisting the insane need to scream. Late-night meetings? Money's worth? *Darn you, Ed Sharp!* she grumbled inwardly. *Why*

*didn't you warn me I'd be spending my days and nights
with this man!*

"Miss O'Conner?" he asked. "Do you feel ill? You
look pale."

She shot him a glance and forced her teeth to unclench.
"I'm fine. And I'm at your disposal—totally."

"If I'm out, and you're not sure where you need to
go, use the phone. As I said, somebody will fetch you."

With a force of will, she pretended to be as free and
easy as he was. "You've got employees who'll come get
me?"

"Absolutely."

She shook her head, confounded. "I've never been a
guest in a house with a taxi service. Wouldn't it be
cheaper to give out You Are Here maps?"

He chuckled, checking his watch. Susan sensed he
wanted to go back to his office. "You'll get your bearings in no time." Reaching around her, he turned the
knob on her door, opening it a crack. "Why don't you
relax. I'll knock around seven and we can go down to
dinner, together. Work will start tomorrow."

She nodded. "I'll be ready, Mr. Merit."

"Call me Jake," he said. After a brief pause, he added,
"And I'll call you…?"

"Oh…" She felt like a dunce for missing her cue.
"It's Susan. Please, call me Susan." She smiled, but
couldn't help feeling a little dejected. Adding her first
name hadn't caused a single glimmer of recognition. He
had no idea who she was. "I'll see you at seven—Jake."
Breaking eye contact, she touched the bedroom door and
it swung wide.

The room that appeared before her was spectacular,
furnished with expensive antiques. Plush blue silk with
emerald embroidery covered the bed and matching head-

board. Yet in some magical way, it seemed surprisingly cozy, bathed in sunlight with bouquets of fresh flowers everywhere. "What is this?" she murmured to herself. "The presidential suite?"

"I refuse to take credit or blame. My mother decorated the house."

Startled that he'd lingered, she spun around. "What?"

"My mother." His eyebrows rose inquiringly. "The one with the eyes?"

He apparently mistook her surprise for confusion. Embarrassed that she's made a remark that he might take as disapproving, she felt an urge to clarify. "I wasn't criticizing. It's fabulous. From what I've seen of your home, it's all exquisite. It just never occurred to me I'd be housed in such formal opulence. Mr. Sharp didn't mention a dress code, so I might not have brought the right clothes. I didn't pack anything dressy." She was babbling and she had to make herself stop. "I didn't mean to insult your mother. Will I be meeting her?" *Shut up! Shut up! Now!*

"She passed away a few years ago. And don't worry about the dress code. You look fine to me."

A peculiar tingle raced along her spine, setting fire to her nerve endings again. *Whew!* She'd had marriage proposals that hadn't affected her as sweepingly as his off hand remark.

When he grinned, a hitch in her heart stopped her breath for a second. "I'll see you at seven, then, Susan."

She felt a shiver of elation at the sound of her first name the way he said it. Susan was such a plain name, but coming from Jake, it seemed special.

Belatedly she nodded her response, but he didn't see it, for he'd turned away. As she watched him stride off, she had the distinct feeling he'd dismissed her from his mind as quickly as he'd dismissed her from his presence. She tried not to feel disappointment. After all, Jake was a busy man. He'd made a great concession taking the time to show her to her room.

She stepped inside and closed her door. By the time she finally expelled a long exhale, her eyes had gone prickly dry.

She rubbed her arm where he'd touched her. The spot felt warm and tickled curiously. "Could I ask one favor, Jake," she mumbled, "before you pick me up—" She glanced at her watch. "—in two hours? It would be helpful if you'd sprout a businessman's paunch and lose a row from teeth."

Susan made absolutely no effort to look fetching for dinner. Well, maybe just a little. After all, she was a professional consultant to Merit Emeralds. She shouldn't look like a homeless person being invited inside for a hot meal.

With a quick peek at her watch, she noticed it was 7:07. One minute later than the last time she'd checked. Perching on the edge of the bed, she could see herself in the dresser mirror. She frowned a warning. "This is not a date and Jake Merit is a busy man. If he said he'd be by to get you for dinner, he will. It's business. The man is *not* pacing around his room trying to figure a way to get out of having dinner with you. *It is not a date!* Get your mind off the word *date!*"

She tilted her head, frowning at herself. Maybe the blue jersey shift and cardigan weren't the best choice, even if they did go with her eyes. The room was the same shade of blue as the outfit. Sitting there dressed all in blue, surrounded by blue, she almost disappeared. If it weren't for her auburn hair and her freckles, she'd be invisible.

She pushed a loose strand of hair behind her ear, wondering if she should have worn it down. With her hair pulled back and twisted in a clip, she looked like a peeled onion. Except for the ends that stuck out like a patch of weeds.

She grimaced. Maybe she should wear it down. Maybe—

A rap at the door made her jump. He was there!

"Yes?"

"It's me."

She bolted up, taking a quick check in the mirror, then frowned at her reflection for feeling the need to do it. "One second," she called.

Rushing to the door, she flung it wide. "Hi..." Luckily she didn't have much of a speech in mind, since whatever she might have added stuck in her throat. He'd changed into a sage cotton shirt and beige chinos, looking scrumptious in his casual, buttoned-down way. She swallowed, hoping he would fill the awkward silence.

"Sorry, I'm late." He stepped back to allow her space to exit. "I had a few calls that kept me busy."

She accepted his wordless invitation and joined him in the hallway. "No need to explain." She closed her door. "I'm sure in an emergency I could have found my way to the dining room."

"Or you could always use the phone and call for help." Inclining his head, he indicated a distant staircase.

"No, I couldn't," she said. "I'm from pioneering stock. Once upon a time, my grandmother found her way out of the Smithsonian Museum, all by herself."

"That was *your* grandmother?" Jake asked, mirth riding his tone.

Susan glanced at his profile. Why did he have to make her feel so—so giddy and contented at the same time? "You've heard of her, then?" she asked, playing along.

"Absolutely. Columbus, Ponce de Léon and Grandma O'Conner. The big three."

She laughed. "But not necessarily in that order."

At the head of the stairs, he paused and flicked his glance her way, his grin wreaking havoc. "Suddenly I feel completely unnecessary."

Though Susan forced herself not to comment, in her opinion, Jake Merit could never be unnecessary. His fingers lightly touching her back urged her down the staircase.

They made a right in the foyer. As they passed an arched entry to the formal living room, a painting over the marble mantel caught Susan's attention. She stopped, stock-still.

"Is something wrong?" Jake asked.

She shifted to look at him. "Sorry." Indicating the living room, she asked, "Is that a Chagall?"

He considered the brightly colored, fanciful imagery, then nodded. "Nice, isn't it?"

"Nice?" She shifted back to stare. "It's wonderful. Mind if I look?"

"Go ahead." He dropped his hand from her back, so she decided he planned to wait in the foyer. It came as a surprise to hear him following.

When she reached the carved mantel, she rested her hands on the cool marble, fighting an urge to run her fingers over the oil painting. "This is a real Chagall," she whispered.

Jake didn't respond, so she faced him. "It's real."

He lounged against the mantel, giving the painting a

cursory examination before turning back to her. "Mom liked his work."

"I've only seen original Chagall oils in museums," she said. "This must be worth hundreds of thousands of dollars."

Once again, he didn't speak. She couldn't help but check his expression. "I have a couple of prints of his lithographs," she added. "Nothing signed or numbered, but I love them."

"So, in your off-duty hours you're an art critic?"

"No—I sketch. I'm not very good, but I recognize genius when I see it."

Her gaze traveled over the dreamlike image of the Chagall. Out of the corner of her eye, she noticed several silver-framed photographs residing on the mantel.

"That's my mother," Jake said, evidently sensing where her survey had taken her. He moved closer. His scent filled her head, making her fuzzy-brained but in a good way.

Susan scanned the photograph. The woman was a pe- tite beauty, with dark hair and huge, green eyes, both praiseworthy legacies she'd left to Jake. "Your mother was very pretty."

"Thank you." He fingered the ornate frame. "I'm afraid she was lonely here, though. The place is so iso- lated—has to be. Decorating the house became her life."

Susan glanced at him and witnessed a glint of melan- choly in his eyes. The sight was so poignant, she had no idea what to say.

When he realized she was watching him, his expres- sion reverted to easygoing nonchalance. "Aren't you hungry?"

"I'm getting there." Behind his shoulder Susan scanned the other silver frame. Larger than the one of his mother, this one held the photograph of a blond woman. She had a fragile ethereal quality about her, an angelic beauty, as though too exquisite for this earth. Susan bit her lip. At last, she was face-to-face with the legendary Tatiana.

It was no secret in Portland, or all of Maine for that matter, that Jake Merit still mourned his fiance, killed the week before their wedding in a skiing accident. To have such an eligible, wealthy bachelor cut himself off from matrimony, was as romantic as it was tragic. The stuff of which legends were made.

Jake shifted, doubtlessly sensing where Susan's focus had roamed. His fingers trailed down the photograph as though in a caress, and Susan felt a perverse twinge.

"This is my—"

"I know," Susan whispered. "Tatiana."

When she looked at Jake, he was staring at the photograph. A look of abject sadness passed over his features. When he flicked his gaze to her, Susan saw pain glittering there. "What?" he said. "I'm sorry. Did you say something?"

She felt a sick sense of loss, which was ridiculous, since this man had never been hers. She'd never even harbored any real hope that he might be. "I—I said, she's Tatiana."

His expression changed to a charming frown of surprise, and she understood why. "Everybody in Portland knows—" she shrugged, indicating the framed beauty "—the story."

His lips twisted ruefully. "Everybody?"

Tatiana's image taunted Susan with its perfection, so she turned away from the mantel. "Surely you're aware that your ill-fated romance fascinates people, Mr. Merit."

After a few seconds of silence, he cleared his throat. "*Mr.* Merit? What happened to Jake?"

She felt silly and didn't know why. Her glance was sheepish. "Somehow, telling you what a tragic figure you are seemed to call for formality."

"Trust me, Susan. It doesn't." He took her arm, both startling and thrilling her, as he conducted her from the room. "Just so you'll know," he went on, "I get five or ten letters a month from silly schoolgirls who've heard the story. They swear their love will save me. If they can call me Jake—which they do—I insist on it from my mining expert. Are we clear?"

Though she sensed her reminder of his losing Tatiana affected him deeply, he appeared at ease. She tried to do the same. Taking a quick breath, she quipped, "Crystal clear, Jake. Or put in mining expert's terms, 'A solid body girdled by natural flat faces that are the outer manifestation of a fixed interior arrangement of intrinsic atoms, molecules, or ions. Particles inhabit—'"

"I get it, Susan," he cut in with a laugh. "You get it."

"I get it, Jake."

"By the way, that was impressive," he said. "Ed never recited definitions to me."

"Inorganic Substance Soliloquies are a new service we offer. No extra charge."

He chuckled, his warm breath drifting through her hair. His light mirth seemed genuine, though she suspected if she looked deeply into his eyes she would witness the haunting specter of his lost love. Feeling as insubstantial as melted ice cream, Susan inhaled for strength. She had a sinking suspicion August was going to be a long month.

CHAPTER TWO

SUSAN found herself sitting at an inlaid-ebony table, so long that, in a crisis, it could have been used as a bridge to the mainland. Besides Jake and Susan, Jake's father, George, joined them for dinner. The three places were set at one end of the long table. The bone china was delicate, the ornate silverware so heavy, Susan decided she could count mealtime as weight workouts while she was here.

She'd never thought of her blue dress and cardigan as particularly dressy, but in such opulence, she felt downright dowdy. George Merit held court at the head of the table in a tuxedo shirt, black bow tie and maroon velvet smoking jacket, looking every inch a king at his leisure.

Sunset had been beautiful, casting a pink glow on everything. Now that it had faded, three lofty, sterling candelabras provided the only illumination. The setting had become troublingly romantic. Luckily for Susan, Jake wasn't there.

Five minutes after they sat down to dinner, he'd been summoned to deal with a managerial issue. So Susan experienced the striking sunset and savored the tart spiciness of the Szechuan fish under the scrutinizing scowl of Jake's father. She didn't enjoy being glared at, but George's stern expression didn't bother her half as much as Jake's grin. Besides, Susan's own father was a scowler. She'd learned years ago that such antics most times consisted of more bark than bite. She had a feeling George Merit's bulldog demeanor could be handled, too.

"Well now, missy, I trust you play chess?"

She glanced at the man to her left. He looked a little like Jake, lacking an inch or two in height and not quite as broad in the shoulders. The major difference, though, was attitude. George Merit was stiff and grim, while Jake was casual and easygoing. The senior Merit's imperious potentate act made it clear that, even though he was no longer CEO of Merit Emeralds, George liked to believe he reigned as king of his island, and would prefer to be called Your Majesty. Susan's contrary side required that she do the exact opposite. "I'm afraid I don't play—George."

The senior Merit sat back, staring at her as though she'd told him to take a flying leap. Rapier-thin and distinguished looking, with his thick shock of silver hair, he looked and acted like a true autocrat.

"How can you not play chess?" he demanded, his tone thundering in the cavernous room. "All professional people should play chess. It exercises the brain, teaches strategy, patience—"

"I simply don't enjoy board games, Geo." She smiled to herself. *Geo.* She was being recklessly impudent. But for some reason, she sensed Jake wouldn't have a problem with it. Susan had no idea why that thought crossed her mind. Maybe it was the way she'd seen Jake treat his father, with casual nonchalance, even in the face of blustery demands.

She smiled at the older man, letting him see he hadn't ruffled her. "For relaxation, I sketch." She knew she should stop there, but she decided she wanted to see his expression when she made her next remark. "As for exercising—both mind and body—I enjoy kick-boxing."

The older man gaped. "A slip of a woman like you? Preposterous." He leaned toward her, eyeing her narrowly. "I've made a decision, missy. You will learn to play chess while you're here. I'll accept no argument."

Susan took a bite of fish, stalling. She didn't know how she was going to handle this, but she didn't plan to get stuck playing chess with George Merit every spare minute. She knew how fanatical some people could be about the game. After she swallowed the bite, she faced him, deciding truth was better than evasion. This tyrant didn't like to hear the word no, so she was going to have to deal with him in a more graphic way. "Actually, Geo, I know how to play chess. I just don't enjoy the game."

"You don't enjoy the game!" he bellowed. *"You don't enjoy the game?"* He slammed his fists on the table so hard the silverware clattered. "Then you haven't been taught correctly. Once I enlighten you to the subtleties—"

"Forgive me, George, but I was playing chess with my father when other little girls were serving imaginary tea to their Barbie dolls." She shrugged dismissively. "I simply have no taste for—"

"Pish tosh!" he interrupted, "Undoubtedly, your father—"

"Is Chester O'Conner," she cut in, curious to see if the name registered.

George stilled in the act of sipping water from a cut-crystal goblet. "The hell you say." As Susan expected, George had heard the name. He thumped the glass to the table, sloshing water. "Did you say Chester O'Conner?"

She smiled sweetly, nodding.

"You can't mean your father is the ranked chess player, *Chess* O'Conner?"

Susan felt a certain pride at his surprise. Her father was world-renowned among chess enthusiasts, and though she loved him dearly, her formative years had

been filled with chess, chess and more chess. Her dad
was the original pain in the neck when it came to insist-
ing his daughters learn—and be the best—at the game.
After she left home for college she'd told him *no more,*
and she hadn't looked at a chess board since. "So you've
heard of my dad?" she asked quietly.

For the first time since Susan met George Merit, he
neither scowled nor bellowed. He sat stunned. She decided to take advantage of this break in his third-degree
to finish her meal.

After a few more seconds, he blinked, closed his
mouth and swallowed. She watched his Adam's apple
pump. "We must play!" His tone was hushed, as though
in the presence of royalty.

Interesting, she mused. *The man who would be king,
or at least be treated like one, now stares at me as though
I were the aristocracy and he the beggar in the street.*
She supposed in the world of chess, she was almost royalty. She shook her head. "No, thanks."

"I insist," he said, his expression stern.

She eyed him levelly. There seemed to be a certain
faction of chess fans who felt that beating the daughter
of a world champion was as good as beating the champion himself. She'd never understood that reasoning, but
if her experiences meant anything, it was rampant.

Generally she found it easy to say no and mean it, but
this case was more complicated. She was stuck on Merit
Island for a month. George Merit was plainly not a man
who took rejection well, if at all. He would no doubt harp
at her, relentlessly. Not only that, Jake was an important
client. Did she dare anger his father? After a long, drawn-
out minute, she nodded. "All right, George. When do
you want to play?"

The older man stood. "I'll get the board set up. Jake

will tell you how to get to my den." With one last narrowed look, he cautioned, "Don't be long, missy."

"Call me Susan, George," she said without smiling. "When you call me missy, I feel like a lapdog."

"Fifteen minutes," he shouted over his shoulder as he charged out of the room. She sank back, wishing she'd told him no, and let the chips fall where they may. She closed her eyes and exhaled, wishing Ed Sharp had explained the living arrangements, and warned her about George's mania for chess.

She'd expected to be set up in some room in a garret or hut, eat with the workmen. Jake would be a far-off, shadowy head-of-state figure, who might wave at the masses from a balcony once or twice to keep up morale. If it was any consolation, she'd been partly right. But it was George, not Jake, who played the part of monarch. She would bet her last dollar George never mingled with the workers.

"All alone?"

She twisted around to see Jake coming through the arched entrance. Her body heated at the sight of him, so tall, with such handsomely chiseled features and that devastating smile. "Your first impression of the Merit men must be very bad, both of us leaving you to eat alone." The rap of his heels died away as he stepped onto the Persian carpet. He passed her, leaving behind his taunting essence. "Where's my father?"

"He went to his den to set up the chess board."

As Jake took his place across from her, he passed her a curious look. "He bullied you into playing?"

She smiled wanly. "He's a hard man to say no to."

Jake made a face as if to wince. "Tell me about it."

"You tell me something." She leaned toward him. "Which would be more likely to turn George off to the idea of ever playing chess with me again—if I'm lousy or if I win?''

Jake watched her speculatively for a minute. "You sound like you think you could beat him.''

The heat of a blush crept up her neck. She wasn't usually so egotistic about her abilities. "Which do you think would make him quit pestering me?''

The quick, brief flash of a Jake's grin was dazzling in the candlelight. "Beat him.''

She'd thought so. It was always the most overbearing challengers who crawled away with their tails between their legs once they were routed. She patted her mouth with her napkin. "Thanks.''

His brows furrowed slightly. "Don't thank me. You haven't won, yet.''

She smirked. "That's true—not yet.''

He watched her as though trying to get into her brain. She hadn't made the most resounding first impression on him. Jake probably thought she was not only goosey around men, but with this latest conceit, very probably deranged. In the silence she watched him watch her. He blinked—twice—and Susan decided scrutinizing the up-and-down movement of his long, thick lashes was quite pleasurable.

"My father's very good at chess,'' he said at last.

She came out of her trance, slowly absorbing his remark. "He made that quite clear.'' She shrugged. "I'll just have to do my best.''

Jake had no way of knowing "Chess'' O'Conner was her father, and since he wasn't a chess fanatic, probably wouldn't recognize the name. She and Yvette had made it a practice not to tell casual dates about their father's prowess at the game, just in case they were chess freaks and might become bothersome about it.

Besides, Chester O'Conner was never one to meet their dates at the door, preferring the seclusion of his den. So Jake had never known Yvette's "dirty little chess secret" as the sisters had laughingly called it. Unless Jake's father mentioned it to Jake, she didn't plan to.

He regarded her with narrowed eyes, and Susan had no idea what might be going through his head. "I wish you luck." He took a sip of coffee, then his lips twitched as though a thought had struck. "I hope you're agile. King George has a penchant for throwing things when he loses."

Susan couldn't recall how many times she'd wished her father had been a world renowned astronaut or maybe a beekeeper. Not that she wasn't proud of his accomplishments, but it would be harder for strangers to pull a space shuttle or a hive out of the closet to challenge her with.

"First he throws chess pieces, then the board. Then anything handy," Jake went on, looking as though he was only half kidding.

"Thanks for the head's up," she murmured.

"It's the least I can do." His gaze was speculative. "I don't like my employees spending more time in a coma than necessary." He took a bite of fish and Susan found herself strangely contented to watch him chew. His jaw muscles bunched and flexed in the candlelight in the most intriguing ways.

She pinched herself on the leg. *Quit that!* she warned. *The man is eating fish, for heaven's sake! It is not a come-on!*

She rummaged around for a safe topic. It was time to get her mind on something besides Jake! "Uh, what was the problem you were called away to deal with?"

He sat back, resting his wrists on the table. The move caused her to notice his hands. They were nice hands, just as she remembered them. Long, tanned fingers and neatly trimmed nails. He wore a gold ring the size of most university class rings. This wasn't a college ring, though. Jake had been a Harvard senior when he dated Susan's sister, so Susan knew what Harvard's class ring looked like. This gold band housed a square emerald, at least five carats. Being a mineralogist, Susan guessed the gem was worth well over fifty thousand dollars.

"It was about sex."

Her glance shot to his face. "Oh—I'm sorry. I didn't mean to pry." Her cheeks burned, but the mortification twisting her insides was a thousand times worse than any physical display. The last thing she wanted to think about—let alone discuss—was Jake's sex life.

He cocked his head and watched her for several ticks of the clock. One eyebrow rose. "I rarely discuss my sex life at dinner." He sat forward and retrieved his fork. "The fact is, there aren't many women on Merit island, and sometimes it's necessary—"

"Please don't make an exception for me!"

He stilled, a forkful of fish halfway to his mouth. "What?"

She swallowed hard. "About discussing your sex life at dinner. Don't make an exception for me."

His lips quirked as though her remark amused him. "You're sure?"

She nodded, longing for her blush to go somewhere and die. It was at times like this she regretted having a redhead's complexion. *Times like this?* she scoffed inwardly. *Susan O'Conner, you've never had times like this!*

Jake lay down his fork. "We're in agreement, then," he said. "Since the reason I was called away had nothing to do with my sex life." Though he'd straightened his features, she sensed that he was laughing at her. "As I was saying, Merit Island doesn't have many women residents. The men—after all, are men. Which is no excuse. Still, every so often, I must straighten out an employee who has had difficulty deciphering the word no. It works best when I, personally, explain Merit Emerald's policy on sexual harassment, and how inelegant a life behind bars can be."

Susan kept her features placid, but mentally gave herself a swift kick. When would she learn to keep her mouth shut and just nod politely? Trying to take her own advice, she nodded politely.

He looked away. When he faced her again, she could no longer detect amusement in his demeanor. "Being an intimidating son of a bitch isn't my favorite part of the job."

A surge of anxiety raced through her at the idea of seeing his intimidating son of a bitch act. "You're intimidating enough when you smile," she murmured, then froze. "Did you hear me say something just then?" she whispered.

Jake picked up his goblet, holding eye contact with her as he drank. A slight frown formed between his eyebrows. After a long, painful moment, he lowered the crystal. "You think my smile is intimidating?"

She tugged her gaze away and eyed the ceiling.

"It's hardly my intention to intimidate you," he said quietly.

She peeked at him. "You don't mean to be intimidating like the sun doesn't mean to shine."

He scanned her face, his expression serious. "You're saying I can't help it?"

"You're tall, you're powerful, you're rich..." She shrugged, embarrassed for having babbled herself into this situation. Why couldn't she babble around George and be courageous and clearheaded around Jake? After all George Merit thrived on intimidation. Why wasn't life fair? "It's not your fault you're intimidating, Jake." She shrugged again. "You can't help it."

He lounged back in his chair, eyeing her thoughtfully. After a minute, he folded his arms across his chest. "And I intimidate you?"

She lifted a shoulder. "Well—in a word, yes."

A male server came in and poured coffee while Jake continued to observe Susan. The long, drawn-out hush was hard on her. Once the young man had gone, Jake sat forward. "You're very honest, Susan."

Her stomach clenched. He'd hit on a distressing truth. She had caught a bad case of brutal honesty as a child, and was never able to shake it. "You say that like it's a good thing."

His quick grin brought new warmth to the room. To Susan's dismay, she experienced an indecent tingle deep in her belly.

From somewhere in the mansion came a chandelier-shaking bellow. Susan reacted with a gasp. "What's that?"

"I believe that's my father requesting your presence," Jake said, watching her with amused speculation.

She swallowed hard. What had she gotten herself into? "Are you serious?"

He rested his elbows on the table and bent toward her. Susan knew he was no more sending off sexual vibes now than he had been while he so seductively chewed his fish—at least not deliberately. Even so, it had its effect. "Would you like me to have a chat with King George about chess harassment?"

She smiled at his dry wit. "Let me try it my way, first."

"If you insist." He watched her for a moment, his expression one of curiosity and concern. "Take some advice?"

She lifted her chin in a half nod. "If you insist."

"King George has a tendency to throw high and to his right," he said. "Lunge left." He winked. "Have a nice game."

Why shouldn't the weather be sunny and balmy? Why shouldn't Jake look scrumptious in jeans and red knit shirt? Why shouldn't *everything* be perfect? Nobody ever told Susan her life would be easy.

But why did even the elements have to conspire against her? Why couldn't Jake be bleary-eyed at seven in the morning? Why couldn't he be a grouch? What was with all that cheerful niceness he threw around?

They talked business as they trekked toward the drilling site over headland rocks, rising above secluded beaches. Susan allowed her attention to wander over the scenery rather than look at the man beside her. Watching him while the breeze toyed with his hair was distracting. Okay, maybe she'd taken *one,* wayward peek. But that would be her only lapse. She'd had a stern conversation with herself last night about her lack of professionalism around him, and she'd promised herself things would change—*drastically!*

Today, she was proud of herself. In every conceivable way she behaved like a professional. She treated Jake Merit the same way she treated every other business associate. With cool efficiency. Flipping through the forms and memos on her clipboard, she kept her mind on business and the conversation on track.

Jake kicked a pebble on the path, drawing her attention to his trekking boots, then up along the athletic contour of his jeans. Luckily he gestured toward something, forcing her attention in the direction he indicated. For the first time she could see the drilling site, still quite a ways away.

"Willoughby only has five, twenty-foot joints of drill pipe for his rig," he was saying. "Is that going to be enough when he has to do those five holes above the cliff?"

She critically eyed the truck-mounted drill. Even from this distance, there was no mistaking it was top-of-the-line. "He can get three more joints from Eddington in Portland, Jake. I was in there checking out the new Christensen core head design last week." She gave herself a mental pat on the back. *Keep it up, Susan, you're doing fine!*

She continued to answer Jake's questions, jotting notes when necessary to remind herself to check on various details. What she did not do was look directly at him. Her attention rebounded off his ear or his chin or his forehead. She had no intention of making any more "you have lovely eyes" bloopers. She was not here to wax poetic about bits and pieces of his anatomy.

"After we've drilled on a tight grid pattern in sector seven, and collected enough samples to analyze— *whoop!*"

A loose cobble underfoot made Susan stagger sideways. Though the trail was a good five feet from the cliff's drop-off, she made a grab for the nearest solid object. After a split second, she realized she'd flung herself at Jake, grasping him about the waist.

Dazed, she stared at his belly. Her legs were splayed out at her sides, her sneakers sliding further and further apart on the loose rocks. Though she was probably more flexible than most mineralogists, letting go would send her thudding to the ground.

She peeked up in time to see Jake's startled expression as he reflexively caught her around the waist and pulled her up so her legs were no longer flared out. "Are you okay?"

Her feet were safely under her, but for some crazy reason she couldn't let go of his middle. She looked squarely into his face. A bad mistake. Mesmerized by his eyes, she could only nod.

"Good."

She inhaled his scent.

"Is there something else?" he asked

My goodness, he smelled heavenly. And he felt heavenly, too. Solid, like a tree, but warm like a—man.

"Susan?" he asked. "Can you stand by yourself?"

She blinked, becoming fully aware that she still hugged him. "Oh…yes…I had a little—spasm in my calf," she improvised. For good measure, she massaged the fake cramp.

"Did you strain anything?"

Just my credibility! "I'm sure it'll be fine in a second." She kept rubbing, unhappy to be bent over, since that made it easier for the blood to rush to her face.

She spied the clipboard several feet away, where she'd flung it. With what she hoped was a believable limp, she took two steps and snatched it. After a count of three, she straightened and turned toward the path, her back to Jake. She had no intention of facing him until the fluorescent glow of her cheeks dulled a bit. More out of nervousness than need, she swiped at her linen walking shorts and embroidered shirt-jacket.

"What was I saying?" Pressing a loose strand of hair

into place, she took a step in the direction they'd been walking. She congratulated herself for remembering to favor her right leg. If she was going to live through that hugging blunder, she would have to fake an injury for a few minutes, then gradually dispense with it as they walked.

"You might have pulled a muscle," Jake said. "Maybe I should carry you."

"No!" she spun to look at him—rather, at the vicinity of his shoulder. She began to suspect she should have put more thought into her face-saving charade. "I'm fine, really."

"Oh?" He sounded skeptical. "Limping is just another service you provide, no extra charge?" He scooped her up in his arms. "I'd better get you back to the house so you can put some heat on that."

"Oh—don't..." She faltered, feeling like an idiot. How could she tell him she'd faked the limp without making things worse? "Wait, Jake." She pointed toward the drilling site. "The truck's already there. So's the crew. By the time we get there my leg will be as good as new." She flailed around in her mind for a way to talk him out of carrying her. No matter how hard she tried, nothing came to mind. *And you know why,* an imp in her brain taunted. *Because being held in Jake's arms isn't exactly making you sick to your stomach!*

"Are you sure you want to go to the site?" The disquiet in his eyes stole her breath. She faced the fact such grisly torment was her due. Why shouldn't lying to save her stupid face bring down more grief on her head?

She nodded, adamant. "I'm positive. I want to go to the site."

With difficulty she shifted away. Refusing to give in to the urge to hug his neck, she folded her arms over her clipboard. She'd done enough impromptu hugging for one day.

"So how did the chess game go last night?" he asked.

She tried not to look at him, didn't want to. She shrugged. "I had to beat him three times to prove the point, but he finally got it."

"No kidding?" He sounded like he was smiling.

Against her will, she peered his way. His smiles were hard to deal with, yet impossible to ignore. She found herself smiling in return. "I think he likes me. None of the pieces he threw even came close."

"Did you lunge left?"

"Always."

His deep chuckle resounded through her, a sensation so pleasant it shocked her, and her smile died. His grin was too erotic. His scent filling her head made her woozy. Unsettled, she cleared her throat. "Put me down, Jake."

"What were you saying before?" he asked, apparently very much his father's son when it came to ignoring what he didn't care to hear.

It wasn't going to work. This was too humiliating. She hadn't let George bully her into endless games of chess, and she was not going to remain in Jake's arms like some helpless infant.

"Look, Jake…" She squirmed, pushing at his chest with an elbow. "The spasm is over. There's no need to carry me." She forced herself to meet his gaze, needing him to see her adamant expression. "This is embarrassing. Put me down."

He halted, surveying her, no doubt gauging her resolve.

She indicated the mining site in a rocky valley below. The workers milled around. Susan felt sure they hadn't

spotted Jake carrying her, yet. "How would you like it
if they saw me carrying you?"

His chuckle rumbled again, making her tingle. She
hated her melting reaction. "That'll be the day," he said.

"You'd be embarrassed." She lifted her chin with bravado. "I feel the same way."

His brows dipped, as if to say, "It's not quite the
same." After a pause when he seemed to recognize she
was dead-serious, he lowered her to her feet. "On the
other hand, I might enjoy watching their reactions if you
carried me down there."

"No, you wouldn't," she muttered, turning away.
"Nobody enjoys looking like a fool."

The morning's drilling went perfectly. Susan was relieved to see the hours fly. She remained so busy, her
idiotic preoccupation with Jake slipped to the back of her
brain. Out of Jake's arms and with him away from her
direct line of vision, she was able to act like the professional she was paid to be.

At noon, kitchen staffers brought out a lavish picnic
lunch. To Susan's relief, Jake returned to his office for a
conference call, so she was free of his troubling magnetism for a while.

She climbed a bluff and ate a tuna salad sandwich,
watching surf glide across a crescent-shaped beach, far
below. The action of the water was calming, and she felt
renewed, refreshed. Almost serene.

Sipping a cola she relaxed on a boulder, absently scanning the mansion, a mile or more off to her left.
Dominating the highest point of land, it was a majestic
sight. The three-story stone-and-timber residence was the
image of an English manor house, commanding a spectacular view. Susan mused, if the Merit family ever tired

of gazing out to sea, there was always the glimmering ornamental pond, complete with sparkling fountain, and obligatory pair of swans. Or acres and acres of sculptured gardens, dotted with statuary and centuries-old trees. It was like sitting in the middle of a fairy tale.

"I wondered where you was."

The guttural voice jarred Susan from her reverie. She jumped up and whirled around, wondering who had spoken. Not far behind her she spotted one of the workmen. Bill or Gil or...she couldn't recall. He was a big man with scruffy whiskers and brawn to spare. She experienced a chill of apprehension, but made herself shake it off. How silly! She smiled politely. "Hello."

He approached, a one-sided smirk on his lips. "Pretty nice view," he said, giving her a thorough once-over. Again the chill of unease raced along her spine.

She swallowed and faced the sea. "Yes, it's breathtaking."

His snicker pulled her attention back. "You're pretty danged breathtaking, yourself."

She experienced a twinge of foreboding. The guy was coming on to her. She disposed of her smile. "This isn't an appropriate conversation."

His grin skewed, became a leer. "No?" He took another step toward her, invading her space. "I think it's plenty appropriate."

His smarmy expression set off alarms she could no longer ignore. "Well, you're wrong. I'm not interested in a date."

He snickered again. "Ya know? You got a cute blush there." He took another step. When she stepped away, she backed into a tree and bumped her head. That made her mad. "Look, Bill or Gil or whatever your name is—"

"Call me Billy." His eyes were small, like shiny black

buttons. He wore a sleeveless T-shirt, streaked with sweat and dust. Big and blond and muscular, the miner was relatively good-looking, except for the beady quality of his eyes. Apparently the ''me-Tarzan-you-Jane'' approach worked for him. Either that or he was wanted somewhere for assault.

She gritted her teeth. "Okay, Billy. Back off."

He took another step, and braced his hands against the tree trunk on either side of her head. "Come on, Susie." His smile was suggestive, nasty. "I watched you this morning. You've been giving me looks."

She stiffened. "Don't make me do something we'll both regret."

He tilted toward her. "You won't regret nothin', sweet Sue. No lady regrets gettin' to know Big Billy."

"This is your last chance to back off."

"Don't be like that, Susie." He dipped his head. "I just want a little sugar for dessert."

"Don't make me hurt you."

He chortled, as though her admonition was laughable. She watched his leering mouth dip toward hers for a count of one and a half more seconds. Two seconds after that, Big Billy was crumpled in a heap, moaning and clutching his family jewels. Susan experienced a stab of remorse for being forced to do that, but squashed it.

Stepping over his barge-size feet, she walked a safe distance away. "Big Billy, you have just learned a valuable lesson about the one and *only* meaning of the phrase 'back off.'"

He eyed her for an instant, his features twisted in pain. Then, with a half grunt, half groan, he rolled over onto all fours, pushed himself up to a crouched position and staggered off. She watched him warily as he disappeared down the slope and around the bend.

The crack of a twig alerted her to another presence, and she spun around, arms lifted in a defensive posture.

"Whoa, I come in peace." Jake stopped short and held up both hands in surrender.

Her heart hammered from her bout with Big Billy. Recognizing Jake, seeing his wry expression, she closed her eyes and expelled a pent-up breath.

"I was coming to rescue you," he said.

She suddenly felt much better. Jake shook his head as though incredulous. "You have some fancy moves, Susan. What was that?"

She felt embarrassed, and didn't know why. She hadn't done anything illicit. "I couldn't get into aerobics in college, so I enrolled in the only thing left open, kickboxing. It turned out to be fun and good exercise, so I kept it up."

His brows rose significantly. "I can see that." He walked over to the tree where she'd recently trounced Big Billy, and leaned a shoulder against it. After watching her for a moment, he smiled. It was a good smile that warmed her. "Let's review, Susan. First, you win prestigious professional awards at—what?" One brow quirked upward. "How old are you, twenty-seven? Twenty-eight?"

She swallowed, confused. "Twenty-eight."

"Right." He crossed his legs at the ankles, looking too marvelous to bear. She forced her attention to hover around his knees. "Secondly, you're the only person to beat my father in chess in recent memory. And third, you punch the stuffing out of two-hundred-and-fifty-pound miners like they were feather pillows." He paused. "What the hell are you looking at down there?"

Startled that he had noticed her reluctance to look him

in the eye, she cautiously lifted her gaze. "Nothing. Sorry." She focused on his neck.

"To put it simply, *you*, Susan O'Conner, are an intimidating woman."

She stared, speechless. Was he paying her back for telling him he was intimidating? Showing her how uncomfortable such a statement can make people feel? If so, the taunt was too subtle. He should be smirking or winking, shouldn't he? Could he possibly be complimenting her? Could he possibly be a little intimidated? *That thought's too crazy even for you, Susan!*

"For the second time in two days you've made me feel unnecessary." The breeze chose that moment to ruffle his hair. The movement caught her attention and she broke her own rule, gazing straight at him—*such a mistake*. The man was lots of things, but nothing close to unnecessary.

Something about his expression was vaguely different. Was it respect she saw glimmering in his eyes? For some reason, she suddenly felt less like a bumbling schoolgirl and more like the capable woman he'd just described. "Don't put yourself down, Jake." She moved to the boulder where she'd eaten her lunch and picked up her sandwich bag. "You can carry this."

He accepted it. "Gee whiz. Thanks."

Light laughter gurgled in her throat. "You're welcome." How charming—this handsome multizillionaire saying "gee whiz" with such boyish charm. It was so irresistible she wanted to reach out and muss his hair. For starters.

When their eyes met, Susan felt as if she'd been struck by lightning. Her brain began to clamor with some insight she couldn't quite grasp. Or maybe she didn't want to. She pulled herself together, ignoring the thing she didn't want to know. Working to appear breezy, she indicated the drilling site. "Let's go, Jake." Swallowing to clear the hoarseness from her voice, she quipped, "Don't make me hurt you."

CHAPTER THREE

THANKS to Jake's assertion that Susan was an intimidating woman, she found herself more at ease. Now that she felt Jake respected her, she did her job flawlessly. The only times she still had trouble were when she and Jake were alone.

At these times, she had to fight to keep from hearing the nagging voice in her head, whispering something she dared not heed. That's why, on the third day of drilling, when the clutch faceplate broke, Susan found herself drowning in a confused brew of emotions. The broken part had to be ordered from Oklahoma, and would take at least three days to arrive. Susan would spend those days around Jake—three days *not* filled with work to occupy her mind.

Still, even as unsettling as this prospect was, Susan couldn't banish her delight at the idea of passing her leisure time around him. Jake was so accessible, so open. He seemed to sense exactly what a person needed and gave it—be it bolstering their ego or lifting their mood. Or, as in the case of Big Billy, a no-nonsense reprimand on How To Behave Around Visiting Female Mineralogists If You Don't Care To Be Prosecuted For Assault.

Susan wondered if a lifetime with cantankerous old George Merit had made Jake into the kind of man he was, having watched his father browbeat and bully all his life. Or had his mother been the model for his heightened sensitivity about people? However it had come about,

41

clearly Jake had chosen a more benevolent managerial approach than his father. Jake didn't rule with an iron fist as his father had—and still did, when he could get away with it. Jake chose to be a good listener and a fair employer, only growing stern when all other avenues had been closed to him.

That night at dinner, George Merit made no mention of the chess games he'd lost to Susan. The subject hadn't come up the two previous evenings, either. As Susan had predicted, George acted as though the incident never took place. Overdeveloped egos fascinated her, and she was glad there were times when she could use them to her advantage.

Oddly she sensed that beneath George's barking he not only respected her but even liked her a little.

Susan excused herself before dessert was served, deciding to take a head-clearing walk in the gardens. She needed to breathe air that wasn't redolent with Jake's scent, to stare off into scenery that didn't include his sparkling eyes or quick, sexy grin.

"*Blast it,* Son!"

Susan stumbled to a halt, unaware that she was practically beneath the dining-room window. She could hear George Merit's roar, clearly. Reflexively she turned, frowning. What was wrong? Old King George, as Jake teasingly called him, had seemed comparatively mellow during dinner—for a tyrant. What had brought on this rage?

"Not now, Dad," Jake cut in. "I'm not in the mood."

"It's going to be now! Do you realize tomorrow you'll turn thirty-five? Do you also realize that when *I* was thirty-five, you were six years old?"

"After shouting it at me a thousand times, even the dinnerware knows it by now."

"Don't be flip!" George shouted. "When are you going to cease your morbid preoccupation with a dead woman and get on with your life? I'm not getting any younger! I want grandchildren before I'm too decrepit to enjoy them." A long pause brought no response from Jake, so George raged on. "As the eldest, you have duties!"

"No matter how you delude yourself, Father, you are not a feudal king. You can't order me to the altar."

"As your father, I have a right to talk sense into you!"

"I'd think you'd be talked out by now."

"Not until I get it through that thick skull of yours that you can't live in the past! Tatiana is gone! Deal with it and move on!"

Susan bit her lip at the mention of Tatiana's name. Under the spell of Jake's easygoing demeanor, she'd allowed the fact of his late-lamented fiancée to slip to the back of her mind. Suddenly weak, she dropped to a marble bench. The chill of the stone made her shiver. Or was it something else, some buried emotion she reacted to?

"*Damn it,* Dad!" Jake said, his tone tightly controlled. "Even if I marry and give you the grandchildren you want, my wife would only have my name, not my love."

"Your love! *Bah!* Grow up, Jake! If you honestly believe no living woman can claim your heart, then any bride will do! Choose one and get on with your life!"

Susan braced her hands on the bench and slumped forward, her buoyant mood evaporating. Jake's statement echoed through her brain—*my wife would only have my name, not my love.*

"No woman would agree to such a bloodless partnership," Jake said.

George's horselaugh filled the night. "You're not a babe in the woods, son. You know most women would do anything, agree to any terms, for the kind of wealth and power your name would provide. Besides, where is it written you have to tell the truth?''

"I wouldn't lie," Jake growled. "Before I'd bring a woman into my marriage bed, I would tell her everything."

"Then you're a bigger fool than I gave you credit for!"

"I'd rather be a fool than a liar."

"You're succeeding admirably," George said, his tone ripe with mockery. "Where are you going?" A booming sound split the waiting quiet, as George slammed his fists on the table. The old tyrant's penchant for slamming his fists on the table was a jarring habit Susan had not quite become accustomed to, no matter how often she'd been confronted with the act. *"Come back here, Jake!"* he bellowed.

No response. Obviously Jake had had enough.

Susan slouched on the cool bench, staring at her shoes. Her mind slipped and slid around, grasping for solid purchase. Once again, her thoughts tried to pry open a door she didn't want to risk looking behind.

Jake Merit, the fantasy of her girlhood and the nice guy she'd grown to know as a client, had damned himself to live alone, with only memories of Tatiana as his companion. What a tragic loss—both to Jake and to some woman out there who might be able to make him happy, if he would open himself up to the possibility. And that woman, whoever she might be, would blossom and flourish in his arms. Susan sensed that as surely as she felt the chill of the marble against her skin. If Jake could only let himself leave Tatiana in the past, where she belonged.

A sound in the distance made Susan turn. Her heart

did an unruly flip to see Jake walking on the lawn. Luckily the bench where she sat was hidden by flowering shrubs.

She shrank back, but couldn't take her eyes off him as he slowed and turned in the direction of the garden. In the moonlight she could see his face quite well. Those chiseled features she marveled at were drawn in grim reverie, his posture that of a stricken man. Yet, he was still breathtaking, even as the half light of night lay bare his brooding hurt.

He ran both hands through his hair in a jerky, frustrated motion that nearly overwhelmed her with an urge to take him in her arms. Comfort him. Give him ease. He blurred, and she swiped at tears that welled in her eyes.

What would it be like to be Jake's wife, bear his children, knowing she could never win his heart? Susan felt a strange stirring in her breast. *No,* she warned mentally. *Don't even think it! You've had all the silly fantasies about Jake Merit any one female should be allotted.*

She watched as he plunged his hands into his trouser pockets and moved to stare out to sea. His back was to her now, but the moon still gave her a great deal worth seeing. His shoulders were broad, capable of bearing great weight. In the white polo shirt, they seemed even more massive, and gleamed like alabaster. He shifted his weight. The curve of a taut hip caught the light. She shivered at the subtle sensuality the move evoked, and hugged herself.

Jake was a compelling presence in bright sun or moonlight, a man she knew to be as self-confident as he was attractive. Yet, observing him from her hiding place, she witnessed for the first time how empty he was. This deep, painful loneliness, self-imposed and possibly hated, was as tangible as the erotic lure of his eyes. Under his free-and-easy demeanor, Jake was a tormented man.

That strange sense of eagerness overtook her again, and she found herself pondering once more what it might be like to be Jake's wife. She grimaced, appalled at herself. Was she crazy? She wouldn't be happy marrying a man who didn't love her!

No! She couldn't even considering marriage under such circumstances! Not to any man in the whole, wide world!

But Jake Merit wasn't just any man.

Jake stared, unseeing, into the dark void. He knew his father was right. How many times had he told himself the same thing? He wasn't living, just existing. He wanted a home, a wife, and children of his own. He'd planned to have all that with Tatiana. But she was gone. She'd been gone for a long time. Twelve long years! How could he have allowed so many days, weeks and months to fall away, denying the passage of time, denying he was even alive. But he was alive. If he didn't snap out of it, he'd find himself a sixty-year-old bachelor who'd let every chance for happiness pass him by.

Was he a lost cause? Was there enough substance left in him to give to a woman? His father was right about another thing, too. There were lots of women who would take him on terms that offered everything to them but love. Didn't he get several letters a week from females who would jump at the offer? But *blast it,* that was no way to pick a wife—randomly from a stack of mail! That could only make a bad situation worse.

What was the answer, then? What were his options? He could choose a life of self-ordained loneliness, which, so far, hadn't given him any satisfaction, much less happiness. Or he could make a compromise that might give him a modicum of both, by offering some woman great wealth in exchange for family and fidelity.

"But who?" he murmured. "Is it possible to buy a wife, yet not damn her for saying yes?"

Susan didn't bring a bathing suit to Merit Island, but the first day of her three-day hiatus stretched before her with all manner of possibilities of accidentally running into Jake if she hung around the mansion. So she decided to take drastic measures. She used her phone and asked the butler if she might borrow a swimsuit from somewhere. Not five minutes later, the courtly gentleman arrived at her room with several beautiful suits, still bearing their tags. It seemed Merit Island was prepared for any emergency.

She picked a blue one-piece, slipped on a pair of sandals, grabbed a towel and headed out of the mansion. The weather was wonderfully warm, perfect for swimming.

"Hey, where do you think you're going?"

She spun, startled by the sound of Jake's voice. He must have been standing behind a tree, because Jake couldn't be visible and be ignored. "I—I'm going swimming," she said.

"Alone?"

He walked toward her, and she found herself placing the towel around her shoulders like a shawl. Some feminine defense mechanism, she guessed. It wasn't that she felt undressed. The suit was respectable. But she didn't like the idea that he might find her body wanting—all pasty-white and freckly. From the picture she'd seen of Tatiana, Susan surmised she'd had flawless, ivory skin, that doubtless tanned to a golden perfection.

"I asked if you were going alone," he repeated, drawing her from her startled doe-in-the-headlights trance.

She nodded. "I'm a pretty good swimmer."

"That wasn't my question." Indicating the ocean with a nod, he came to a halt, once again just outside her personal space. His scent wasn't as civil, as it stole around her. She breathed him in. "Don't you know you're asking for trouble swimming alone?"

Feeling like a chastised schoolgirl, she scrambled for some excuse that didn't include how hard on her it was to be near him. "I—I guess I figured you had security cameras that would monitor me, and somebody would come to my rescue before I went down for the third time." She grinned, trying to appear flippant, but inwardly she wanted to crawl in a hole. It was beginning to look like she should have stayed in her room and read.

"Come to think of it, you're probably right about the rescue." He waved an arm toward the distant wood. "Over the hill, there's a sunny cove where the water's warmer. Wait a sec and I'll go with you."

She hoped she hadn't heard right. *"You?"* she squeaked.

Jake had turned away, but shifted back. "Why? Don't you think I can swim?"

She shook her head to clear it.

"That's not very complimentary." His brows knit, though she had a feeling he wasn't all that bothered by her seeming lack of faith. "You're not the only one with talent around here. At Harvard I was on the swim team."

"I know," she murmured.

"What?"

"I said—oh," she lied, tugging the towel more securely over her breasts.

"Wait right here."

Before she could respond, he'd turned away.

She watched him disappear into the mansion. For an eternity she stood there, chewing on her lower lip. Why did it seem the Fates insisted on harassing her? He was more troubling than Big Billy could ever hope to be.

Jake emerged from the mansion and, as he jogged in her direction, she smothered a groan. He was all fluid motion, all male animal. His green swimsuit rode low on trim hips, and though the suit was baggy and almost knee-length, she was as blown away by the sight as if he'd been naked. He exhibited way too much taut, tan flesh for her to deal with calmly.

"This will be fun." He came to a power-stop that caused so many muscles to tense and bulge her breath caught. "I'm glad you had the idea, Susan. I haven't been swimming in a long time."

She forced a smile. "Goody for me."

With a casual hand at the small of her back, he urged her along. "Did you know today was my birthday?"

She adjusted her face to look surprised. "Oh?" He didn't need to know how she'd found out. "Happy birthday, Jake. What does a birthday party for Jake Merit look like?" she asked, trying to keep the conversation light, and her mind off the warmth of his hand through her swimsuit. "Let me guess. You're having some Broadway show shipped out here for the evening. Or are you flying in some star-studded production from Las Vegas?"

His chuckle was wry. "I haven't had a party since I was eight."

She stared at his profile, his firm mouth, curved upward as though on the verge of laughter. But now she knew how false that carefree face was, and her heart twisted.

"But you get gifts, right?"

He glanced her way, his expression skeptical. "What do I need?"

You need to find happiness, Jake. She bit her lip to keep from blurting that out. She shrugged. "I didn't know I'd be here on your birthday, or I'd have brought you something." She winced. What a silly, smitten-schoolgirl thing to say! She decided to cover with a platitude. "It's not the gift, it's the thought that counts. Everybody needs a little attention."

"That's a nice sentiment," he said, then flashed a grin. "Why don't I consider this swim your present to me?"

She watched him but couldn't speak as his smile did its melting worst.

"You'd think somebody who lives on an island would remember to go swimming once in a while," he said, evidently discarding the birthday talk.

"You're a busy man." She clutched her towel and wondered what excuse she might use for keeping it bundled around her while she swam.

He looked away, scanning the ocean. "Yeah. That's me. Busy."

She peered at him. His expression was reminiscent of the way he'd looked last night when he'd thought he was alone. After only a split-second, the sadness was gone. When he shifted back, his expression was the good-humored mask he showed to the world. "It doesn't look like you swim much, either."

"It doesn't?" She cleared the squeak from her voice. Why couldn't she have grabbed one of those huge bath sheets? Her towel simply wasn't up to the job of hiding her.

His glance roamed over her, then returned to her face. "You're very pale."

Heat rushed up her neck, heralding another furious

blush. "Well, you're *not* pale, and you say you don't swim." She wasn't sure there was any logic to her response, but sound reasoning wasn't her biggest concern at the moment. Watching Jake take mental inventory of her body—then come up with the less-than-flattering adjective pale—*was*.

He looked away. "Touché, Miss O'Conner."

"If you don't swim much, how do you get so tan?" His hand continued to warm her back through the fabric of her swimsuit. It was difficult to keep her mind on track.

"I run."

This surprised her. "I haven't seen you."

He flicked her a glance. "Maybe you haven't been paying attention."

I doubt that! She managed to keep from scoffing aloud, but only by the intervention of some alert guardian angel with quick reflexes. The declaration had made it all the way to the tip of her tongue before she managed to bite it back.

"Tell me, Susan," he said, "you say you're a pretty good swimmer?"

She nodded. Wondering at the subject change. "Pretty good."

"What about kick-boxing? How good would you say you are at that?"

"Pretty good," she said, wondering where he was going with this.

He lifted his chin in a half nod. "Ah."

"Why?"

"I was trying to decide whether to challenge you to any swimming races."

"Oh? So, do we race?"

His dark eyebrows arched mischievously. "Not in a million years."

Susan sat silently at dinner that evening, not quite following the track of conversation as her mind trailed stubbornly back to that afternoon and her swim with Jake. She couldn't remember when she'd had so much fun. He'd been overly humble about his ability as a swimmer. Jake was powerful in the water, with a butterfly kick she couldn't have matched in a thousand years.

He'd also been the epitome of all that was gentlemanly, never touching her beyond the light hand at her back as he guided her to the sunny lagoon. Susan found herself wishing he'd been just a little bit—what—something?

"Interested" was the word that loomed in her mind. But that would have been wrong of him. After all, he had hired her firm as professional consultants. In a very real sense, she was his employee, at least for this month. Sexual harassment was a big concern to him. If he lectured guilty employees, then turned around and treated his women employees the same way, he would be nothing more than a hypocritical weasel.

Still, was it sexual harassment if it was consensual? Her head shot up from her dinner plate, and she gasped aloud. *Where was her mind?*

"Is something wrong, Susan?"

She blinked, remembering where she was and how her foolish gasp must have seemed to Jake, his father and their two other dinner guests. She swallowed. "Nothing. I just—bit the inside of my cheek." Okay, so it was a lie. But if ever, in the history of the world, a lie had been necessary, this was it.

The sound of a titter brought Susan's attention to the

only other female at the table, a rosy-cheeked, tidy woman of around sixty. Emma Fleet had been introduced to Susan as the wife of the island's resident doctor, Elmer. "I hate it when I bite my tongue," she said in her scratchy-soft voice. "Once you bite it, seems like you keep nipping it for days." She turned to the tight little knot of a man beside her. Though small and wiry, his cheerful personality made him seem more substantial. "Elmer does it all the time, poor dear." She patted his age-spotted hand. "Don't you, El?"

The old doctor smiled, his sharp brown eyes full of kindness and good humor. "You'd think a doctor'd know better."

Susan smiled. Dr. Fleet and his wife were completely genuine. They reminded Susan more of a simple country doctor and his wife rather than the personal physician of the great and powerful Merit family. Susan was pleasantly surprised to find them at the dining table when she arrived. Jake's charisma and George's scowling stares were unsettling, each in their own way. The major downside was that Jake now sat on Susan's right. Several times their hands brushed when they both reached for the cream. She vowed silently to start drinking her coffee black.

For some bizarre reason, George was doing some serious staring, tonight. Every time his glare pinned her down, she wondered what she'd done to make him take special, glowering note of her? Had she misread him? Had he been boning up on chess, preparing for a rematch? Was he about to spring another challenge on her?

George cleared his throat importantly. A shiver of foreboding slithered along Susan's spine. She felt certain he was about to enlighten them about whatever had been weighing on his mind. Well, the answer was no. She placed it on the tip of her tongue, ready for the challenge when it came.

"Susan," he barked, canting to stare directly at her. "So, what are your plans for the future?"

"No!" she said firmly, then frowned. That hadn't sounded like... "What?"

"No?" George shouted. "What kind of an answer is no? Are you saying you don't want to get married someday?"

Confused, she shook her head. "No...I mean...yes. I hope to get married and have a family, one day."

One stone-gray eyebrow lifted. "A family." He nodded. "Children. Excellent. I—"

"Say, Doc," Jake broke in, "How's Martenson? I understand he broke a rib in that fall."

"Yep." Elmer's laugh was high-pitched and crusty. "Danged freak thing, falling off his top bunk onto Weidermeir's head." He patted his lips with his napkin, his chortle percolating deep in his chest. "Weidermeir didn't even get woozy. That old reprobate has a head like a bowling ba—"

"If you don't *mind?*" George interrupted, eyeing Jake with displeasure. "I was making a point."

"I mind," Jake said.

Susan flicked a startled glance toward Jake, surprised by the severity of his tone. A muscle bunched in his jaw, and he eyed his father narrowly, as though telegraphing a silent warning.

"Come now, Jake," his father barked. "She's beautiful. She plays chess like the devil, and she knows emeralds. How about it? You and Susan could give me exceptional grandchildren."

Susan's bite of salmon took a painful detour to her lungs.

CHAPTER FOUR

FURIOUS and helpless, Jake watched Susan's coughing fit. He knew better than to pound her on the back, so he waited and worried and boiled, ready to jump in with the Heimlich if need be. After about thirty tense seconds, she sucked in a breath of air. So did Jake and everyone else at the table. At least, Old King George hadn't added manslaughter to his list of misdeeds.

Over the years, Jake had heard his father bellow some rash and tactless things, but this marriage proposition was beyond inexcusable. "Father, what in blazes did you think you were—"

"Susan, dear girl!" George cut in, grasping her hand. "Give Jake an heir, and you can *have* a quarter of Merit Island. How about it?"

Jake's anger mutated into white-hot fury. "Be careful, you old tyrant," he ground out. "Susan is dangerous when riled. I wouldn't blame her if she kicked you out a window."

When George opened his mouth to speak, Jake glared a threat. Surprisingly the old man closed his mouth. With a huffy flourish, he busied himself patting his lips with his napkin.

Jake turned his attention to Susan. Her astonishment, and quite possibly her recent lack of oxygen, had siphoned the color from her face. He couldn't blame her for being horror-stricken. Experiencing a rush of empathy, he pushed up to stand. "Susan..." He cleared his throat, doing his best to wash the fury from his tone. "I apologize for my father."

A few heartbeats later she stirred, evidently gathering her wits enough to register that he'd spoken her name. She faced him, her eyes shimmering ovals of humiliation. The sight turned his rage at his father's bullying into a living, breathing beast, and he had to struggle to maintain control. His instinct was to grab old King George by the shirtfront and shake the daylights out of him. He tried for a reassuring smile. "Would you like to go to your room, Susan?" He offered her his hand.

The movement caused her to shift to stare at his outstretched fingers. For several seconds she sat very still, then suddenly lay her hand in his. Her touch was ice-cold. "Thank you," she whispered.

He assisted her from her chair, then gave a nod to the doctor and his wife, across the table. Elmer and Emma sat openmouthed. If the situation hadn't been so appalling, their expressions would have been comical. "You'll excuse us, Doc? Em?"

The couple continued to stare. Jake peered narrowly at his father. "I'll deal with you later."

George snorted. "If you're smart, you'll close the deal with Susan first."

Jake's glare remained fixed on the senior Merit. "*Try* to stagger into the twenty-first century, Dad—where the couple makes the decision to marry, and meddling fathers stay the hell out of it!" He squeezed Susan's hand. "Let's get out of here before I indulge in some well-deserved patricide."

Susan lifted her gaze to Jake's face. Though her expression was pained, she managed a smile. "Do you need any help?"

He felt the impulse to laugh and was amazed. Even as

the victim of King George's most contemptible tampering in Jake's memory, Susan O'Conner had not only survived, but had done so with her spirit intact.

Susan couldn't recall a more ghastly moment in all her twenty-eight years. She'd had fantasies about marrying Jake, true, but not at the request of his father. She recalled Jake's eyes after hearing the proposition. Even narrowed in abhorrence they were striking, but the memory of his annoyed reaction unsettled her. The idea of marrying her was plainly not at the top of Jake's Things I'm Dying To Do list. If she could make any judgments from his expression, the notion wasn't even in hot contention to be added to the bottom. Never in her life had she felt a more overpowering urge to be swallowed by a crack in the earth.

"Susan, I'm so sorry." Jake's apology pulled her from her musings. She became aware that they were standing in the hallway outside her room. "I don't know how I can make up for what my father did." He shook his head, looking charmingly contrite.

"It wasn't your fault," she said, trying to appear poised, as though the incident hadn't been crushingly humiliating.

Jake leaned against her doorjamb, clearly unhappy. He winced at some thought and closed his eyes. His long, thick lashes swept down to brush his cheeks. The only sound for several seconds was the whisper of his heavy exhale. When he looked at her again, his eyes glimmered with regret. "Maybe it would help if I explained."

That brief glimpse of his vulnerability was wildly sensual and she felt weak. To keep from sagging to her knees, she slumped against her door. "It isn't necessary to explain. Forget it."

She reached for her doorknob, but was startled when he caught her fingers in his. "Yes, it is. You see, my father thinks I should—"

"You don't have to tell me, Jake," she said. "I—I heard the argument last night. I was walking in the garden." Experiencing a twinge of guilt, she smiled wanly. "I didn't mean to eavesdrop."

Jake's lips twisted ruefully. "It's not eavesdropping when the decibel level of our father-son chats could shatter windows at the far end of the island. My head-butting with Old King George is legendary."

Susan was touched by his honesty. She knew about head-butting with stubborn, pushy fathers, herself. Rarely had she come away from a difference of opinion with her dad—especially if it took place in front of witnesses—able to make light of it. "Fathers can be fun, can't they?"

"Yeah." He released her hand and crossed his arms over his chest. "Since you know my problem, may I ask your opinion?"

She nodded. Clasping her hands together she tried to ignore the way her fingers tingled with the memory of his touch.

"Susan, would *any* woman marry me—under the circumstances?"

The straightforward inquiry caught her off guard. She forced herself to remain outwardly placid, but on the inside she scrambled to form a coherent thought. She hoped *she* wouldn't marry him under the circumstances, but she couldn't make any promises. There was no doubt in her mind, however, that thousands of women in Portland, alone, would shout yes at the top of their lungs. She decided to answer his question with one of her own.

"Would you want *any* woman—under the circumstances?"

Jake's brows dipped and he appeared to ponder her response. "No," he finally said, averting his gaze. "Not just any woman." When their eyes met again, he added, "I'd like to think, with the right woman, I could make a good marriage. Build a family. Find—" He stopped himself. "I can't believe I'm talking with you about this."

She couldn't believe it, either, but it was nice having Jake confide in her. "I don't mind. If I can ever be of help, just…" She shrugged, feeling silly. Telling Jake to come to her for assistance was like suggesting the king seek counsel from a peasant. "Ask me," she finished, lamely.

"Thanks." He continued to hold her gaze, and she experienced a fluttery stirring. She didn't understand what his eyes were saying, but it didn't matter. The intensity and beauty of his stare was so riveting, so awe-inspiring, it was worth her time, even if she had no inkling of what might be going on inside his brain.

"Would you, Susan?"

His question confused her. The silence in the hallway became awkward as she stared, puzzled. "Would I—what?" she asked.

He shifted his attention, staring off into the distance, then frowned as though trying to think of the right words. When he looked at her again, a charming flush crept beneath the tan of his face. "Marry me?"

He'd spoken so softly, Susan wasn't sure she'd heard right. Even so, her breath froze in her lungs and somewhere deep inside, hope flickered like embers on a cold hearth. "Would—would you repeat that?" she whispered.

Watchfulness etched his features. "I said, would you marry me?"

Her heart leaped erratically, as though caught up in some New Age ballet. *She had heard him right!* She gulped several times, making a valiant effort to tamp down her panic—or was it excitement? Anticipation? The fulfillment of her dreams?

No! she counseled sternly. A loveless marriage isn't the fulfillment of any woman's dreams! She battled to keep herself in check, to be rational, to stuff her crazy, fanciful desire for him, and keep her head on straight. With mammoth effort, she got a grip on her emotions. "You're asking me hypothetically—as a woman in general?" she asked, needing the clarification to get her heartrate under control. She hoped she sounded analytical and self-possessed, though her face felt stiff. "I mean—" She shook her head, trying to clear a peculiar wooziness from her brain. For a second there it seemed like—looked like you were proposing marriage." She bit her lip. Why, oh why did she have to say that out loud?

He took her hand, and bent slightly toward her. "I think—I was." Gently he squeezed her fingers. "It's a solitary life, here on Merit Island. But for the right woman, it could be a good life." His smile was gentle, but held no hint of passion. That knowledge tore at her heart. "My father may be a self-centered brow-beater, but he was right about not letting you get away. You're smart. You know emeralds. You're good company." His lips twitched in a lopsided grin. "You don't take guff from my father, and you can beat the tar out of him at chess." He sobered. Any doubts she might have had about how serious his proposal was, disappeared with his smile. "We'd make a good team," he added, seriously.

"Team?" she echoed. "We're people, Jake, not oxen."

He winced. "I didn't mean—I meant to say, I believe we could make a good home together."

For a few foolish seconds she actually considered the notion. Those wonderful eyes, that deep, coaxing voice, his arousing scent. Jake possessed a deadly charisma. Add to that the fact that he'd just murmured a list of her attributes—even taking into consideration he'd put her knowledge of emeralds before the fact that she was good company—the mix took its toll on her good sense.

Sadly, beneath all his striking good looks and persuasive charm, she detected a guarded reserve. Whether she wanted to acknowledge it or not, a barrier stood between them and any possibility of true happiness.

Tatiana.

The portal Susan had so desperately barricaded in her subconscious, suddenly burst wide and the secret she'd caged in her mind flew at her with a ferocious roar.

She loved Jake Merit.

A lung-constricting grief overwhelmed her. She had been in love with him from the moment she opened the door to her family home and saw him standing there— so tall, with his indolent, king-of-the-jungle grace, and drop-dead grin.

Her unconscious love for him had shaped her life. Jake was the reason she hadn't been able to commit to marriage. Jake was even the reason she'd become a mineralogist—in her subconscious need be a part of who he was, what he did, even remotely.

Suddenly many things she'd never been able to explain to herself or to anyone else were all too clear. *She was hopelessly in love with Jake Merit—and he'd just asked her to marry him!* So, why wasn't this the happiest day of her life?

"Are you thinking about it?" Jake asked softly, breaking through her thoughts.

She blinked, coming back. Heavens! He was waiting for an answer! An answer to a proposal of marriage! Misery washed over her. *I love you, Jake,* she cried inwardly. *I've always loved you. But if I agreed to this, I would be cheating us both.* With a slow shake of her head, she whispered, "I don't accept proposals from men whose daddies force them into it."

His brows knit in a slight flinch. He took her hands. "I know it seems like the idea was my father's. But he only made me see what was right in front of me."

His warm hands clasping hers was a cruel maneuver, making it hard to think, or breathe. Her heart constricted with longing. What would she have said if he'd given his proposal more than a minute's thought? What if she'd never heard him argue with his father? What if he didn't insist on excruciating honesty and she didn't know he wasn't in love with her?

Such what-if games were useless. Like it or not, the unvarnished truth was part of Jake's deal. Unable to stand the sweet torment of his touch, she tugged her hand from his grip. "Your father isn't the only one I have an urge to kick through a window!"

Jake regarded her pensively for a moment. After a few tense heartbeats, he cleared his throat. "That's a no, right?"

A frustrated moan issued up from her soul. Grabbing her doorknob she twisted until it unlatched, then pushed into her room.

"Susan, wait..."

"No!" Spinning around, she poked his chest with a finger. "Don't make me hurt you, Jake!"

Taking a brisk step back, she slammed the door. The last thing she saw was his face—and the clench of his jaw. Or had it merely been distortion caused by welling tears?

Underneath Jake's blasé guise, he was curiously disconcerted. It wasn't merely male pride, either. When Susan slammed her door, he experienced a weird sense of loss. "That's stupid, Merit," he muttered. "Shake it off."

Susan O'Conner was a capable, attractive business associate—if disquietingly homicidal, at times. As far as the Merit men were concerned, she had valid reasons for her fury.

He stalked into his room and dropped to the edge of his bed. His attention caught on Tatiana's picture. She smiled up at him from his bedside table, all blond-angel-sweetness, just the way she was when he'd met her on that fateful vacation in Paris.

Tatiana had been a stunning combination of French and Russian parentage, a descendant of cast-out Russian royalty, and every inch a princess. He'd loved her madly from the moment they met.

He skimmed his fingers down her face in a caress of sorts, a gesture that had become reflexive. Sitting back, he rested his hands on the bed, but didn't remove his glance from the image in the silver frame. "Where would you be now, if I had been the one who..." He grimaced, reliving the pain of losing her. "I hope you'd have been more intelligent than I've been, Tati. I hope by now you'd be happily married, with children."

He gritted his teeth and looked away. "I can be a

world-class idiot when I put my mind to it." Weary, he
lay back and stared at the ceiling. "You should have seen
me tonight."

He closed his eyes, another world-class move in idi-
ocy, since all he could see was Susan's face—her eyes
glistening with tears as she slammed her door. "Yep,"
he muttered, derisively. "Congratulate yourself, Merit.
That marriage proposal was a world-class jackass move.
I'm surprised she left you breathing."

He muttered a curse. Okay, so he'd taken a shot and
it misfired. No big deal. He ran both hands through his
hair, peculiarly troubled. "No big deal," he mumbled,
figuring hearing it aloud would convince him.

Susan didn't jog. The last thing she wanted to do was
jog. Well, second to last. The very last thing she wanted
to do was be within sight of Jake when he did. So, naturally, the first thing the morning after Jake's offhand
proposal, she saw exactly that. She'd decided to take a
book outside and find a cozy spot in the garden to read.
As she ambled across the lawn, Jake came into view.
Wearing nothing but black running shorts and shoes, he
raced over the grass, toward her, flaunting his body.

It flashed through her mind to jump behind a tree, but
he waved, making it apparent that he'd spotted her.
Clutching the book to her breast, she leaned against a
gnarled oak. She plastered on a thin smile. Since he was
running, her struggle for composure would only be necessary for a few seconds. Then he would be gone.

To her great distress, he came to a halt before her.
Morning sunlight touched his torso, the sheen of exertion
highlighting and defining well-toned muscle. His con-
toured chest expanded as he took a breath. "Hi," he said,

then bent forward. Placing his hands on his thighs, he sucked in air.

She pressed her back into the tree to give herself a millimeter more distance, though he wasn't crowding her. There was just something about him, that made him seem physically nearer than he was. After a couple more deep breaths he straightened and flashed a stunning smile. Brief but potent.

His perusal took in her firmly clutched copy of *Emma* along with her lettuce-edged T-shirt, short trouser skirt and chunky platform sandals. A provocative tremor skated along her spine at his slow perusal, and a wayward scamp inside her hoped he approved.

"A romance, huh?" When his eyes met hers they exhibited a teasing twinkle. "I'd have thought you'd prefer something like the biography of Atilla The Hun."

"I've read it," she said, trying to appear as nonchalant as he did. "Not enough violence."

A deep chuckle warmed the morning crispness as he reached for her book. His fingers grazing her collarbone was enough of a jolt to allow him to pluck the novel from what had been a death grip only a second before. He turned the book in his hand, giving it an amused once-over, then held it out to her. "Did you have a nice breakfast?"

She accepted the book and returned it to its position as a shield. Working to avoid looking at parts of him that might inflame her, she focused on an ear. "Actually—I wasn't very hungry." In truth, she was afraid she would run into him, and she couldn't face him. She'd been rude and ugly and she was ashamed of herself. A polite no would have been sufficient last night. Besides, sooner or later she'd have to eat, so her decision to forgo breakfast was childish.

"I didn't eat, either."

Her gaze snapped to meet his and she winced at how stupid that was. Those eyes made a twisted mess of her emotions.

His wonderful emerald glance searched her face. "Hungry now?"

She swallowed, and lowered her gaze, too unsettled about last night's proposal fiasco to deal with looking squarely into those eyes. She lifted a shoulder in a shrug. "I hadn't thought about it."

"What if I have some food sent out?"

She experienced a pinprick of self-recrimination. She should have known Jake would be gracious about her overreaction. After all, he had no emotional investment in his proposal. He'd made the offer openly, honestly and seriously. She shouldn't have exploded the way she did. "Don't have anybody trouble themselves about me," she said. "I'm fine."

"There's a coincidence."

When he didn't go on, she looked up, confused. "What's the coincidence?"

"I'm fine, too." He winked. "See you later."

He moved away and Susan stared after him, perplexed. His "I'm fine, too," remark didn't make sense. And the wink? Aside from short-circuiting her breathing, it hadn't had the slightest effect on her. "Not the slightest," she muttered, watching as he rounded a corner and disappeared from view.

Twenty minutes later, Susan sat in the sunshine on a grassy spot beside a gurgling fountain. Deeply engrossed in the novel, she was startled when something nudged her foot.

"Hey, there."

She looked up to see Jake towering above her. He'd

obviously showered, since his hair was still damp and he'd changed clothes. He wore beige shorts and a copper-colored knit shirt. And he held a covered basket.

As though he'd been invited, he settled on the grass beside her. "How do you feel about apple and cream cheese coffee cake, tomato quiche, a ham roll, orange juice and coffee?" He lifted the basket lid, pulled out a checkered tablecloth and unfolded it. With a snap of the fabric, he spread it before her.

Bewildered, Susan watched him lift out a thermos. "Coffee first, or juice?"

"What are you doing?"

He unscrewed the cap on the thermos. "I missed breakfast, so I thought I'd eat."

"And you came out here to do it?"

His grin flashed, crooked and sensual. "Don't be obtuse, Miss O'Conner. I could hear your stomach growl ten feet away." He lifted out a mug and filled it with steaming coffee. "I was a jerk last night." He held the mug toward her "Can you forgive me—and eat?"

The inviting scent of strong coffee wafted up and she eyed him levelly. "You were a jerk, you know."

"Ouch." He winced. "And, if you'll notice, I'm trying to apologize." He pressed the mug closer. "Don't starve just because you can't stand the sight of me."

She accepted the brew, and exhaled, releasing with that breath any lingering hard feelings. The man was impossible to resist. She took a sip. "I wasn't exactly the queen of charm, myself." She shook her head. "I'm sorry I was such a shrew."

He poured himself some coffee, then leaned back on one hand and took a drink. "I'm grateful you didn't cripple me."

He smiled, and she had no choice but to smile back.

"Bosses I cripple tend not to give me my Christmas bonus."

"How narrow-minded." He watched her, his grin now full-fledged sexy.

Laughter gurgled in her throat and she felt a light-heartedness she shouldn't let herself feel. "And you're not narrow-minded?"

"I didn't say that." He stretched out his legs, his calf brushing her knee. "I just happen to believe you're not going to cripple me."

She eyed him speculatively. "I'm not?"

He rattled his coffee, a smile lurking at the corners of his mouth.

"You're sure about that?" she asked, enjoying their little game, whatever it was.

"No, but…" He lay his mug on the cloth and lounged back on both elbows. "I'm an optimist."

She laughed, outright, and shifted to sit on her feet. "Oh, you are, are you?"

He nodded. "There's a lot to be said for optimism."

"Okay, Mr. Optimistic, what did you say you have in that basket?" She leaned over his long tan legs, giving herself an instant of guilty ogling pleasure, before she began to forage for food. "I'm starving."

"So, Susan, why aren't you married?"

She jerked to stare at him. "What?"

"I asked, why you aren't married?"

She sat back, her face heating in a furious blush. "That's none of your business."

A brow rose. "Come on. My private life has been laid bare for you. It's only fair you share a little of yours with me."

"No, it's not."

He laughed. "You're one tough customer. Okay, I'll have to assume nobody's asked."

"Yes, they have!" She bit her lip. He'd taunted her into that, the shrewd bum!

He lifted his chin as though skeptical. "Really?"

She eyed heaven. "Okay. I've broken two engagements. Satisfied?"

His brows dipped. "Have trouble with commitment, do we?"

She glowered at him. "We do *not!*"

He angled to face her more fully. "You're sure?"

He was inching too close to a truth she could never allow him to know. Making a quick grab for the basket, she hefted it over his legs. An instant later, it thudded to the grass on her side of his legs. Whirling to put her back to him, she dug in the hamper. "I think I'll try some of that quiche."

"So did you not show up at the church, or did you give the poor beggars a little notice?"

She gritted her teeth and kept fishing around. A pan of quiche came into view. Thankfully it was precut. She grabbed a slice and a linen napkin to put it on.

"I should be grateful you turned me down flat," he said, as though he had her complete attention. "You saved me the humiliation of being left at the altar."

She took a huge bite of the quiche and chewed. It was probably delicious, but she couldn't taste it. She had to swallow several times to get it down.

"Considering your history with men," Jake went on, casually, "what do you think it would take—"

"*To get you to shut up?*" She twisted around to impale him with her most savage scowl. Unfortunately she underestimated the vehemence of her spin and ended up sprawled on top of him.

Shocked by her unexpected collision with his body, she could only blink and stare.

To her great dismay, Susan was compelled to note how painfully gorgeous Jake looked up close and personal, his tempting lips barely a handsbreadth from her own. How tormentingly good he felt, so solid, so male, beneath her.

Most disturbing of all, however, was the way Jake stared back. To say he was shocked by her impromptu, full-body attack would be laughingly inadequate.

CHAPTER FIVE

JAKE'S lips were slightly open, as though crashing down on him had caused him to forcefully exhale. She didn't doubt that, since she wasn't exactly a snowflake.

A need to push up and roll away scurried through her consciousness, but it didn't linger long. Some wayward part of her brain drew her unrelentingly to focus on his lips. Firm, masculine lips slightly parted, as though in blatant invitation. Lips she'd fantasized about for so many, long years. Suddenly so accessible. Just an inch away. One, insignificant inch.

She relished the feel of him beneath her, and the titillating warmth of his breath against her mouth. Her instinctive response was so powerful, so all-consuming, she could no longer ignore her crazy, undisciplined need to know the taste and texture of his mouth, his kiss. With an almost imperceptible tilt of her head, she angled her face toward his.

An instant before their lips met, she felt more than heard him clear his throat. "Susan," he whispered, his voice a husky whisper.

The way he spoke her name, with the vaguest hint of question and perhaps a touch of caution, brought her back to reality with a slap. She snapped her gaze to his face. His eyes, those bright green angel eyes, had narrowed, long lashes masking anything she might have read in his glance.

"Susan, I..." He started to say more, but whether out of civility or confusion, didn't go on. His lips thinned for an instant and his lashes came up so that she could once again read his eyes. His gaze glimmered with reflected light, and something else. Was it yearning? Uncertainty? Oh Lord, could it possibly be pity? "Susan, we…" He winced and gritted out a low oath.

"Oh…" She cried, belatedly realizing the awkward position she'd put him in. His stand on sexual harassment in the workplace wouldn't allow him to toy with a colleague, no matter how wildly she might fling herself at him—however accidentally.

"Oh—I'm—" Mortified beyond words, she slid her hands to the grass and tried to straighten, but nothing happened. Clearly her mutinous body wasn't ready to relinquish their intimate connection. "I can't, uh, my arms won't…" She made a pained face, appalled at herself for the absurd weakness any contact with his body caused her.

Some bleak emotion came and went on his features. He clamped his jaws, seeming to gather himself together. She sensed he'd had a flash of Tatiana, of some situation like this—only there had been no need to hold back. The memory obviously caused him pain.

"Let's see if I can be—" he cleared his throat, again "—of any help." Shifting slowly to one side, he turned them both until she touched grass and rolled to her back. He leaned over her, supporting himself by placing a hand in the grass on her other side. "Breathe," he said, his expression troubled. "You'll get your breath back in a minute."

Did he really think she'd had the breath knocked out of her? Or was he saying that to be gracious. Either way, she opted to go along with it and took a deep breath. Unhappily his scent was a huge part of the process. She stared up at him, taking him in as he hovered, so close, yet so excruciatingly distant.

"Better?" he asked, his expression serious.

She nodded, biting her lower lip. What an idiot she was. Unable to bear his detached solicitude, she cast her gaze away.

He didn't roll away, which surprised her. After a moment, she felt his fingers gently graze her brow, moving her hair off her face. "I've never known anyone who blushed as furiously as you do," he said softly.

She swallowed with difficulty. Unable to keep from looking at him, she turned back. "It's a glandular problem," she muttered. "I'm taking pills."

His lips twitched at her quip. "What a terrible misuse of medication." Their gazes locked for another beat before he firmed his lips together and sat up. Extending his hand, he asked, "Feel like sitting yet?"

He took her wrist. Against her will, she thrilled at the warm strength of his hand. "Thanks." Once she was sitting, she made herself pull from his grasp and looked away. "I'm—I'm sorry about falling on top of you."

"No problem," he said. "I'm used to it."

She flicked him a glance, and he winked, the bare beginnings of a smile curving his lips.

"You are, huh?" She crossed her arms before her, trying to ignore the way she still tingled from their body-to-body contact. "Women fall on you a lot, do they?"

"Almost daily. It's an occupational hazard. Emeralds seem to make women dizzy."

"Poor, poor man. I had no idea." She eyed him with skepticism, but in truth she wouldn't have been surprised—except that there were so few women on the island. "It must be exhausting digging out from under all those females."

"Crippling." His smile teased and titillated as he turned away to check the basket. Reaching in, he brought out a piece of quiche. "It's recently come to my attention that you get cranky when you're hungry. Now, *eat* before you do me real damage."

She continued to frown at him, but deep inside she was grateful that he was making light of the whole awful episode. Sadly the incident weighed heavily on her, and she didn't feel a bit well. She shook her head. "I'm not hungry."

His brows dipped. "Shut up, Miss O'Conner, and open your mouth."

He held the wedge of quiche toward her. "Open those lips or this will end up squished all over your face."

"I don't want it," she insisted. "Don't be a Pushy Jughead!"

He lowered the pie, his expression one of wry amusement. "What is this, insubordination in the ranks?"

"Shocking, isn't it?"

A brow rose. "What happened to the Susan O'Conner who swore I intimidated her?"

"Never heard of her." Though she tried to be flip, she felt woozy and insubstantial. She didn't dare attempt to stand, so she had no choice but to sit there. It was just her bad luck that his thigh was flush against her hip.

His expression playfully stern, he tossed the slice into the basket and lounged back on his hands. Crossing his legs at the ankles, he scrutinized her. After a while, he asked, "Since I've lost the ability to intimidate you, and you refuse to eat, should I brace for round two?"

She had to give him credit, he recovered quickly from the trauma of almost being kissed by one of his work force. She shook her head. "I think I'm through attacking you for today."

He was too near, his scent and the pull of his gaze too potent. She needed distance and she needed it now! With a mammoth force of will, she scrambled away to a position where the basket was between them.

She watched Jake eat a roll. Watched him chew, his eyes trained on her. "Pushy Jughead?" he mused aloud. "Where have I heard that before?"

She inhaled sharply. He'd heard it from her when she'd called him that, once, long ago. They'd been sitting in the parlor of her parents' home. Making conversation while waiting for the eternally tardy Yvette to come downstairs, he'd asked her about her boyfriends. Since all she dreamed of was Jake Merit, she'd blurted defensively, "None of your business, you Pushy Jughead!" He'd laughed, then gallantly agreed that he was beneath contempt to intrude on her private life. She winced at the memory of her childish petulance. She would have preferred that Jake had remembered her, but not because of that.

He looked thoughtful, no doubt reaching back in his mind. "I'm sure somebody called me that once."

"Well, *duh!*" she retorted with bravado. "I'm surprised everybody doesn't call you that!"

His lips quirked. "I walked right into that one, didn't I?"

She fought a grin but lost. "It was too easy. I'm ashamed of myself."

"I can see that." His brows remained knit in thought for another second before his expression cleared, as though casting off the mystery as insignificant. He nodded toward the food in the basket. "Go on. As your host I insist that you eat."

She passed him a dubious look. She felt less woozy now that there was a basket between them.

"Okay, Miss O'Conner, if you want to be weak from hunger, it just gives me the advantage."

His comment confused her. "Advantage to do what?"

He swallowed another bite. "Bob and weave."

She couldn't hold back her laughter any longer. Shaking her head at him she bit into a ham roll. It tasted delicious. "This is good," she said.

"Just one of the many services we offer. No extra charge." He reached into the basket himself. "What about that quiche?"

This time, when he offered her a piece, she gave in and took it, careful not to brush his fingers with hers. "Thanks, my first slice went flying someplace."

"Into the fountain. I imagine the tropical fish are confused. They don't usually get quiche until Saturday."

She cast a quick, worried look toward the shimmering geyser nearby. "Oh dear, do you think it'll hurt them?"

His low laugh brought her attention back to his face. "That's great. You worry about the fish but you don't even ask how I am after your brutal assault."

She rested a hand on the checkered cloth and gave him a long, slow look, starting at his loafered feet and moving languidly up his body to dark, breeze-ruffled hair. If she could have made her perusal any briefer, she would have, but she couldn't help herself. Gazing openly at Jake was an indulgence she rarely allowed herself—at least not in long, leisurely blocks of time. When she finished her survey, she inhaled a shaky breath. There wasn't a thing about him she would change. And there wasn't a thing wrong with him. He looked as healthy as a horse—a stud. She cringed inwardly, pushing back the risqué thought.

With a look she hoped telegraphed indifference, she refocused on his face. "You don't look well, Jake."

His chin came up slightly, as though she'd whacked it with her fist. "Thanks. I work at it."

"You're quite welcome." She finished off the ham roll and decided she was thirsty. Being this close to Jake made her throat feel peculiarly dry. "Didn't you say there was orange juice in the basket?"

He nodded. "I'll get it."

"No, in your weakened condition, I wouldn't want you to trouble yourself." She grasped the container at the same time he did. "I said *I'll* get it." She jerked the container from his grasp, causing the flip-top spout to fly open. Cold juice sloshed over Jake's lap.

"For the love of..." He jumped to his feet.

"Oh!" Susan sprang up, too. "I'm sorry. I didn't mean..." As she gestured, more juice flew from the plastic container, splattering Jake across the face and chest.

He yelped as the icy liquid doused him. "I can't believe you did that," he said, wiping his eyes with the back of his hand.

Susan was pretty appalled to discover that, herself. "Oh—dear..." She dropped the quart container, now practically empty.

Running a hand through his hair, Jake scattered orange droplets in the breeze. "I suggest you run, Miss O'Conner, " he warned.

"What are you going to do?" she cried.

"You're going to find out—if you're not fast." He took a step in her direction.

She had a sinking feeling she wasn't—at least not as fast as he was. The instinct for self-preservation didn't require great logic, so she pivoted away, and headed for the sea. Jake had mentioned the nearby cliff was his favorite diving spot, so she ran for it. If luck was with her, a shark would devour her before Jake could get his orange juice soaked hands around her throat.

"It was an accident!" she yelled over her shoulder, kicking off her cumbersome sandals as she fled.

"I'd suggest you save your breath and run!"

She sprinted with all her power, racing madly toward the drop-off. The water below would be icy, but being hauled into Jake's arms, no matter how harmless the game, would be too reminiscent of things she could never truly have.

A hand snagged her waist, but she bounded away just in time, and plunged over the cliff.

"*Susan!*" he shouted. "What the hell..."

Those were the last words she heard before the frigid Atlantic swallowed her whole.

Instantly chilled to the bone, she paddled to the surface. This was far from the first time she'd been swimming in the nippy Atlantic, so the cold water was as familiar as an old friend. Treading water, she sucked in a breath and peered upward. Fifteen feet above her head, Jake stood on the cliff's edge. Fists planted on his hips, his legs braced wide, he was a breathtaking sight—tan, powerfully built...and angry. She waved and smiled. "Was that fast enough, Jake?" she called. His annoyed expression didn't ease.

"*That* was stupid!" he shouted.

"Not as stupid as almost allowing myself to kiss you," she muttered, then louder, she added, "I'm a big girl. I know what I'm doing."

"Susan, get out of there. You just ate! Do you want to get stomach cramps?"

She pushed dripping hair out of her face. "Maybe!" she shouted, irked that he was treating her like a five-year-old.

He said something that she couldn't make out, but she had a feeling it wasn't a congratulatory speech about her intelligence. The next instant he executed a flawless dive, splitting the water with hardly a ripple. She made a face. "Yes, I know. You were on the Harvard diving team, too."

He came up not far away and shook water from his face. "Are you insane?"

"Thanks, I'm fine." All of a sudden the ocean seemed awfully crowded. She turned her back on him and began to swim toward a granite shelf that extended into the surf. "I'm cold," she threw back. "I think I'll get out."

"You're damn well right you will."

She shifted to peer at him, annoyed by his authoritarian attitude. "On second thought, I've decided to swim a while."

His expression closed in a scowl. "Think again, Miss O'Conner."

Experiencing a flutter of apprehension at his intimidating tone and the ominous glint in his eyes, she turned away. "On second thought..." She had a feeling she'd better move her tail toward shore as fast as humanly possible. He looked like a man bent on retribution.

She switched from a casual breaststroke to a racing crawl, flutter-kicking her heart out. She was a good swimmer, but she'd never been on any swim teams. On the positive side, she was nearer to shore than Jake, with a couple of body-lengths head start.

Panting and sputtering, she reached the granite outcropping. Her arms trembled from exertion as she clambered onto the solid, if slippery, ledge. Once safely out of the water, she allowed herself a smile of triumph.

A strange, churning sound caught her attention.

Shifting, she saw Jake, all glistening muscle and taut flesh, rising from the sea amid a sunlit torrent.

She was struck dumb by the sight. Poseidon, himself, couldn't have made a more exhilarating show, ascending from his ocean kingdom. *Poseidon,* she mused, *the god of the waters, earthquakes—and horses.* The word stud surfaced again. Susan grew furious with herself for her inability to keep this man's mere nearness from punching all her erotic buttons.

"Okay," he said, straightening to his full height. "How do you want it?"

She peeked up at him, her heart fluttering foolishly at the vision he made towering there. He was the image of a Greek god, glinting with a million silver droplets, his broad shoulders nearly blocking out the sky. Except Jake Merit was the revamped, New Millennium notion of what a really hot Greek god should look like.

His shirt stuck to him, which made for an impressive sight, as his chest expanded and contracted with his deep breaths. Clearly he'd been challenged in their race. But that was little consolation, now.

Making a disgruntled face, she turned away from him and settled on the outcropping, her feet dangling in the cold surf. "If I have a choice of j-juices to be doused in, I prefer apricot." She set her chattering teeth. *Let him dig that out of his shorts.*

"You're freezing."

"No I'm n-not!" She shivered and crossed her arms before her. Only then did she realize Jake's shirt wasn't the only one with the capacity to stick to its wearer. Her T-shirt was plastered to her skin, leaving nothing of her feminine attributes to the imagination. She'd never been more thankful she'd turned her back on a man. "Whatever you're going to d-do, do it and go away!" she shouted, hunching over. She couldn't feel her feet any longer, and she didn't think that was a good sign.

His low, sardonic chuckle drifted above her, the rich sound prevailing over the rumbling surf. Curious, she twisted to look at him. He stood there, tall and gorgeous, eyeing her with dark intent. He shook his head in apparent incredulity. "Before today, I never had the experience of watching a woman jump off a cliff to avoid me."

"No?" His dratted smile, even cynical as it was now, could fire up an extinct volcano. A willful thrill skittered through her, making her furious with herself. "Maybe you should get out m-more."

He bent toward her and slid an arm around her middle. "Is advice concerning my social life another free service you offer?" His lips grazed her ear as he spoke. "No extra charge?"

The stirring feel of his arm encircling her beneath her breasts, coupled with the sensual brush of his lips on her skin, shocked her into speechlessness.

A millisecond later he hauled her off the ledge. She gasped as the world went topsy-turvy. In the next instant she found herself deposited across his shoulder like a sack of meal. "What do you think you're doing?" she cried, breathless.

He began to trudge up the rocky slope. "I'm rescuing you from a watery grave."

"What—*ugh*—watery grave! I was fine!" She swiped at the back of her skirt, hoping it was long enough to hide all the essentials.

"That's not how I plan to tell it."

She slapped at his back. "Put me down! I don't want any security cameras shooting up my skirt!"

"I wouldn't worry about it. They're probably still wiping away tears of laughter from the orange juice caper."

She resented his high-handedness, and she resented how helpless he made her feel. There was so much about Jake Merit she resented! But what she resented most of all, was the way he'd stolen her heart without even the common courtesy of knowing about it! "Jake Merit, you're—you're a *beast!*"

"Just another of the many services we offer, ma'am. No extra charge."

"Oh—*you!* Put me down!" She squirmed and waggled her legs, but he held her firmly about the knees. "I'm not kidding, Jake! *Put me down!*"

"You're not completely saved yet!" His deep-timbred voice was resolved, leaving her no hope for release.

"*Jake,* if you don't put me down, this second, you're a dead man!" Her warning was lame and they both knew it. There was little she could do from this position but pound his back and turn red in the face.

"What's wrong? Can't you beat me to a pulp from that position?"

"Not without a concussion, I can't," she muttered.

"Evidently, kick-boxing has a few flaws."

"Oh, you—*you Pushy Jughead!*" Embarrassed beyond words, she redoubled her pounding. "For your information, this position doesn't come up much!"

"That's a shame."

As suddenly as she'd been hefted off the rocks, she found herself tottering in soft grass. Jake's hands gently gripped her upper arms, steadying her. When their eyes met, they were very close. Too close. His dark, brooding expression unnerved her.

Her emotions were in such turmoil, she fairly vibrated. Why must she feel the need to smack him across the face *and* leap into his arms, pleading for his love? Furious, she brushed his hands away. "I did *not* throw that juice on you on purpose, and you know it!"

His jaw worked for a moment as he grimly surveyed her, trembling before him. After what seemed like an eternity of strained silence, he took a step back. Dragging a hand through his hair, he exhaled heavily. "You're right. I'm sorry, I don't know what…" A harassed look came into his eyes and he flinched. "I'd—uh…" He plucked at his shirtfront by way of explanation, peeling it off his chest. "I'd do that, if I were you." His voice low and rough, he turned and began to walk away, muttering, "We wouldn't want to inflame the servants."

Waiting for the replacement part hadn't been the long, drawn-out waste of time as in past, similar situations. Of course, in the past, Susan O'Conner hadn't been on the island straddling his middle, tossing orange juice in his eyes or leaping off cliffs to avoid his touch. All in all, the element of frustration and annoyance he usually felt when work stopped had been less due to the delay, and more because of an undue measure of awareness of Susan O'Conner.

As he walked back from checking over the drill site for tomorrow, he bit off a curse, recalling Susan's face when he'd left her standing in the grass after their chilly dip, yesterday. A lightning strike of shock had flashed in wide, blue eyes. Such charming rosy humiliation blossomed under her freckles it was almost impossible to turn and walk away. He shook his head. "Get your mind on your job, Merit, and off the water-soaked image of a co-worker with fiery, freckled cheeks."

Susan had kept her distance the rest of the day, and this morning, too. She'd asked for breakfast to be brought to her room. With a deep inhale, he plunged his hands into his trouser pockets. "Well, what did you expect her to do, Jughead?" he grumbled.

He frowned, some scrap of memory teasing him for an instant. Jughead. The phrase "Pushy Jughead" came back to him. Where had he heard that before?

A sound attracted his attention and he absently glanced toward it. When he realized what it was, all other thoughts evaporated. Down a gentle slope, through some trees, Susan appeared in a clearing. He walked a few steps down the incline and lounged against a stunted oak. She seemed to be exercising. No. More like sparring, but by herself. She executed kicks and blocks and punches at dead air. Scrutinizing her movements, he ran a hand through his hair to smooth it off his forehead.

Jake had never been an enthusiast of kick-boxing, so he didn't realize such lethal pivots and punches could look like ballet in the hands—and feet, and arms and legs—of a graceful woman.

He watched her do some kind of spinning kick, impressed by how much power she could pack into her delicate stature. He pursed his lips, deciding the word "feminine" didn't necessarily mean "weak" these days. Neither did the phrase "you play like a girl," which could very well turn out to be a goal many men should aspire to. He closed his eyes and rubbed them, marveling at his peculiar train of thought.

After an indeterminate amount of time idling there, it occurred to Jake that hanging back in the shadows like a fainthearted suitor was foolish. He took a step toward her, then, stilled. Suitor? He frowned at his unexpected choice of image. Is that how he saw himself, as her suitor?

He watched her for another moment, troubled. She was lovely, bright and capable. She knew emeralds, and she knew mining....

He bit back a curse, recalling how he'd grabbed her like some kind of latter-day Tarzan and tossed her over his shoulder. He couldn't imagine what had possessed him—indulging in such idiotic behavior—especially since he insisted on a harassment-free workforce and gave lectures on the evils of caveman behavior where female co-workers were concerned. Yet there he was, throwing a woman—a professional consultant—over his shoulder like some kind of lusty Neanderthal.

He clenched his jaws, recalling his reaction to their impromptu romp. He'd felt extraordinarily alive, covered in orange juice, plummeting off the cliff, and most especially during his weird, machismo pilgrimage up the slope, her body, all soft and firm at the same time, draped over his shoulder...

His gut tightened with the provocative recollection. *Blast!* How long had it been since a woman made him feel like a living, breathing man. Like Tarzan, able to swing from jungle vines, his woman slung across his shoulder, as he carried her to their hut where he would make wild, crazy...

He shook himself. "That's enough!" he gritted through clenched teeth. "So, Merit, if she makes you feel like that, what are you going to do about it—besides stand around daydreaming like a bashful schoolboy?"

He surveyed her as she jabbed and feinted, kicked and punched. His mind fumbled around. The answer he wanted lurked there, but he had some difficulty admitting it. "You're going to marry her, that's what you're going to do." He straightened his shoulders and shoved both hands through his hair, his decision made. If her first rejection had related to Merit Emeralds, he would have discounted it out of hand. He wasn't a man to take no for an answer in business, so why should he meekly accept it in his personal life? Which was more important?

He might not love Susan in the deep and abiding meaning of the word, but she did things to him, filled his senses, made him feel alive. These were significant things—things he hadn't felt in a very long time. These new sensations she excited in him were so strong they were almost disturbing. Though it wasn't love, it came close, and might even make up for the one thing she could never be to him.

The word betrayal flashed through his mind, and he recoiled. His thoughts turned to Tatiana, but he shoved the guilt back. Tatiana was gone, but he was alive. Yesterday, for the first time in a long while, he'd actually felt that way. "Damn it, I want to live," he growled. "I want to be a fully functioning man, again. With Susan, I believe I could be."

His resolve solidified like a rock in his belly. Though still determined not to lie, he vowed this time he wouldn't burden her with brutal honesty. Subtlety would be his watchword. His pursuit would be discreet, a masterwork of cunning persuasion. "Brace yourself, sweetheart," he whispered, "your days of abandoning fiancés at the altar are over."

CHAPTER SIX

"So, I MIGHT inflame the *servants,* huh?" Susan kicked out at the emptiness, wishing a certain scowling, dimpled *Pushy Jughead* was there taking the punishment he deserved. How dare he embarrass her that way!

That's not why you're mad, an annoying inner voice nagged. *You're mad because Jake Merit wasn't inflamed! You are a sick puppy, Susan! Or should I say lovesick?*

"Don't say anything!" she grumbled, ferociously pummeling the poor defenseless air. *"Just shut up!"*

"I didn't say a word."

Visions of Big Billy sprang to her mind, and she spun toward the voice, planting herself in a defensive position. When she saw Jake, a jumble of emotions attacked her at the same time. He was so big, so powerfully built. His hair fluttered engagingly in the breeze. With his hands slipped casually in his pockets, he moved toward her. She ping-ponged back and forth from white-hot resentment to sizzling arousal.

"Whoa there, killer." He raised his hands as though in surrender. "I was just passing by and thought I'd say hello."

She eased out of her battle stance and turned away. She needed a few seconds to regain her composure, so she walked to where she'd left her water bottle and towel. Sweeping the jug off the ground, she squeezed out several swigs, pausing between each to inhale a calming breath. When she replaced the jug beneath the tree, she made herself face him. "Hi." She swept hair out of her face then indicated the direction of the mansion. "Have a nice day."

He crossed his arms before him, a clear indication he had no intention of taking her broad hint. "Who were you beating up?" he asked. "Or do I need to ask?"

She eyed him, crossing her arms over her chest. Though she seemed to be mimicking his stance, the move had more to do with yesterday's "inflamed" remark. She was uncomfortably aware that her exertion had caused her sleeveless T-shirt to cling to her. "You'd have to be a very poor guesser to be wrong."

His eyebrows rose. "That's what I thought."

She had a sudden, crazy idea. "You could make up for yesterday by doing me a favor."

He surveyed her speculatively. "I draw the line at killing myself."

She smiled wryly at him. That dratted charisma could reach right out and smack you across the heart. "Okay, Plan B." She indicated the center of the clearing. "Be my sparring partner."

His brows knit and he watched her with high skepticism. "Oh, since I won't kill myself, you'll do it for me? Gee, thanks."

She felt her anger melting and her ardor growing. Jake was a cruel man, making her have such a rough time remaining righteously indignant. "I don't want to kill you, Jake." She walked to him and curled a couple of fingers behind his belt buckle. Why she did that, was anybody's guess. She certainly didn't plan to think about it. Tugging him forward, she tried to appear tough and all-business. "Don't be a pansy," she said, her tone deliberately goading. "I just want you to stand there so I can have a target."

He grimaced. "Oh, fine. I'm reassured."

She planted her fists on her hips. "I'll pull my punches."

"What about your kicks?"

She made a face. "If it'll make you feel better, block."

"Block?" He inclined his head as though he'd never heard the word before.

"Yes, block." She punched at his midsection. In a flash, his forearm cut across his torso, deflecting her attack. She gave him an I-knew-it look. "Like that."

"Oh—that. "

"Yeah." She backed up a step. "Ready?"

He made a pained face, but his eyes twinkled. "Are you sure in a minute you're not going to be running away shouting, 'It was an accident'?"

She pulled her lower lip between her teeth, not happy with the reminder, and shook her head.

"What was that? I couldn't quite hear you."

She passed him a grumpy look. Experiencing a surge of peevishness, she thrust her leg at his chest, like a battle lance. With amazingly swift reflex action, he blocked her.

Startled, but impressed, she nodded. "Good job."

His brows dipped. "That didn't feel like you pulled your punch much."

With a quick grin, she sliced the air with a side kick that he avoided by bobbing to the side. She wagged her brows at him. "You're quick."

"I prefer that over dead." He slashed such a heart-stopping smile, Susan's breath caught in mid-inhale. Feeling awkward, she glanced away to get herself back in control. "You're doing..." She cleared the squeak from her voice. "You're doing fine."

A few more thwarted kicks later, she backed away and held up a halting hand. Unusually breathless, she pushed back stray strands of hair. She didn't generally get this

out of breath after so few kicks. Pivoting away, she
trudged to her water bottle and took a swig. As she was
about to lay it down, she had a thought. "Would—
you…" She straightened, holding out the plastic jug.
"Are you thirsty?"

Wiping his forehead with his arm, he nodded.
"Thanks."

He took the bottle and drank. When he lowered it to
give it back, a startled look came over his features.
"Where did you get boxing gloves?" He sounded wary,
like a mouse happily chomping cheese, only to suddenly
spy the trap slamming shut.

She tugged on a glove. "They were under the towel."

He tossed the bottle onto the grass. "Oh, good. I was
afraid we were done."

Wayward laughter gurgled in her throat. "Keep your
guard up, Jake. I'm going for your nose."

He lifted a hand to his face. "I don't recall any woman
saying that to me before." He eyed her with mistrust.
"What has my nose ever done to you?"

*If he only knew! His nose, his lips, his eyes, his hair.
They all did things to her! Unruly, diabolical things, that
kept her tossing and turning at night!* She looked at him
askance and lied in self-defense. "A broken nose would
give your face a little character."

"Just out of curiosity, what kind of mangling would
give my face a lot of character?"

She fought a grin. He was evil inflicting his easy charm
on her. Lifting her glove, she touched his ear. "First, I'd
pound this baby into cauliflower. Maybe chip a couple
of front teeth. Then, as the coup de grâce, leave a big
scar where one eye used to be."

"That's all?" he kidded.

She managed to keep a straight face. "Sure. With a

battered old face like yours, it wouldn't take much.'' Hoisting her gloves, she resumed her fighting stance. "Ready?"

He raised his arms in a defensive position. "Go for it, champ." He winked. How such a minuscule act could seem so brazen was beyond Susan. Still, it nearly undid her.

Hauling in a restorative breath, she smashed her glove straight at that darkly fringed, impertinent eyeball.

He turned her punch aside with hardly a flick of his wrist.

She punched again. He deflected her with minimal exertion and seemingly little heed. His eyes remained on hers, his grin taunting.

She kicked, and he veered out of reach.

Another kick, and he swerved away from danger. Her initial astonishment at his nimble reflexes moved to admiration. She hadn't met many opponents as fast on their feet.

She punched and he bobbed. After a time, confusion replaced admiration. Was this guy human?

She aimed her next punch at his cavalier grin, but he easily deflected her try. Her mood veered as sharply as he did, and irritation overwhelmed her. She struck out with a kick, and he parried with a low block.

Muttering to herself, she jabbed at his belly, but he sidestepped. This was getting ridiculous. She'd never hit so much *nothing* in all her sparring experience.

She kicked, he deflected, his grin never altering or dimming.

Susan's temper flared. How dare he laugh at her! How dare he never even let her lay a glove on him. Drat the man and his breakneck reflexes! The infuriating, dodging son of a rat! *She was good at this. So why couldn't she land one lousy punch?* "Wait a minute! Wait a minute!" She held up her gloves. "This isn't working. Go ahead and defend yourself."

"I thought that's what I was doing."

"No—I mean *attack* me."

His chuckle was derisive. "Right."

She glowered. If there was one thing she would do, it was wipe that grin off his face, or her name wasn't Susan Faith O'Conner! "I'm serious, Jake."

His smile gradually disappeared. Stepping back, he dropped his arms to his sides. "You can't seriously want me to punch you."

Annoyed by his chuckle, she drilled him with a glare, "Only if you *can*."

"But, Susan, I don't want to hit you."

"Then kick me." Her expression warned him of the dangers of saying anything that vaguely smacked of head-patting.

He started to respond, then closed his mouth. She watched as his jaw worked. "Like hell, I will."

Her exhale bordered on profane. His remark wasn't precisely head-patting. It was more painfully straightforward than that. "That's exactly my point," she said. "You won't be able to hit me."

"I don't have any gloves. If I connect it will hurt."

"What are you worried about—your fist or my body?"

His brows dipped. "That's very funny. Nevertheless, breaking your jaw is not what I had in mind for this afternoon."

She motioned him forward. "Come on. If you're squeamish about hitting a woman, you may pull your punches."

"Oh, *may* I?" he asked, his tone scoffing.

His attitude unsettled her. Everything about the man

unsettled her! "Defend yourself, sucker." Exasperated, she jabbed him hard in the solar plexus.

On impact, he made a grunting sound and hunched over. When he looked at her, his eyes were shuttered. "Thanks—" he gritted, "—for pulling your punch."

Her initial surge of triumph abruptly shriveled, and her cheeks went fiery. She'd been so annoyed, she hadn't softened her punch at all. "I—I'm sorry." She backed up a step, half expecting quick and harsh retribution. "But—I warned you to defend yourself."

He straightened. "Right." Lifting his fists to their former defensive position, he nodded. "It won't slip my mind again."

She bit the inside of her cheek. Far from proud of herself, she lifted her gloves. "Ready?"

His lips twitched, and she experienced a shiver of apprehension. "Anytime, Brünhilde."

Confused, she cocked her head. "What's that?"

"*She* was a mythological female warrior."

Feeling oddly complimented, Susan had to force herself to keep her expression grim. "Ready?"

A brow rose, the green fire in his eyes teasing. "You already asked me that."

"Okay—right…" Her face flaming, she readjusted her stance. What was her problem? *Move it or milk it, Susan!* "*Okay!*" she shouted, jabbing at the flat of his belly.

Instead of deflecting her jab, Jake grasped her wrist. Before she knew it, she was slammed into him. She let out a high-pitched gasp. How did she get here—pinned breast to chest with Jake, both her arms imprisoned behind her back? Arched into his body as she was, she could only stare in surprise.

"How'd I do, champ?" he asked softly.

His chin touched her forehead, his breath feathered her

hair. She had to arch backward to get a clear view of his face. In that precarious stance, she was even more in his control. "What exactly was that?" she demanded weakly.

His grin was crooked, rakish. "I don't know. It just felt right."

She gulped hard. It didn't feel so bad to her, either, but she struggled not to be affected. "I can use my knee from this position," she said, wishing the warning hadn't come out quite so breathy.

As he watched her face, his smile mellowed somewhat, though his eyes continued to plague her with their teasing. "Isn't using your knee against the rules?"

"The way you're holding me is *not kick boxing!*"

"It isn't?"

She gritted her teeth. "You know it isn't! It's not even wrestling! It's more like kidnapping!"

His chuckle rumbled through her, making her breasts tingle. She squeezed her eyes shut. The last thing she needed was to start tingling.

"I never said I was a kickboxing expert, Susan."

She wriggled, too late aware that rubbing against him was ill-advised. It only gave her a greater physical range for gathering information about the man she was plastered against. An unwarranted moan of longing issued from her throat, but she covered with a cough. Jake Merit might not be an expert at kickboxing, but he knew something about how to hold a woman.

"What do we do, now?" he asked, his lips grazing her brow as he spoke.

She blinked, dazed. Had he teased her with his lips on purpose? She focused on his mouth, each intake of breath growing more and more difficult. She craved the feel of his lips against hers. She'd craved his kiss, dreamed of it, yet despaired of ever tasting such bliss. Frightened, she felt her resolve slipping.

Kiss him, you fool! she told herself. *Don't let this chance pass you by. Look at his expression. He's not smiling, now. He's seriously considering kissing you. Take whatever he'll give. How many chances does a person get in one lifetime to live out a fantasy?*

Though she tried not to, she found herself sinking into his embrace, relishing his arms around her, his clean, manly scent. She looked up, actually lifted her chin. *Traitor!* she admonished inwardly. *Don't do this!*

All amusement gone from his expression, his stare was seductive and intense. He fairly radiated a heady sexuality that was hard to resist. His head canted slightly, ever so slightly in her direction, and she experienced a surge of excitement. The air snapped and crackled with the power of his charisma. She was slipping fast. In mere seconds she would no longer be able to resist the wordless lure of his gaze, and that realization frightened her.

What about tomorrow, Susan, she cried inwardly, *when you both go back to work? And speaking of work, how much longer will you have this plum job if you give in to your need? You're not a woman who lives for the moment. You've always had a good head on your shoulders. Don't jump off any sexual cliffs now, no matter how heady the fall!*

How ironic life could be. Jake had offered her a loveless marriage. Now it seemed he'd replaced that offer with an unspoken invitation for casual sex. What a tragedy that the only thing she wanted from him would never be part of any deal he might lay on the table.

The silver-framed photograph of Tatiana flashed in her mind, and anguish washed over her. Jake might not be a snarling bully like his father, but was this playful seduction any less shameful? Her throat aching with misery, she struggled against her desire for him. "Let go of me. Jake," she cried brokenly. "You don't fight fair."

The new clutch faceplate arrived on schedule, core-hold drilling resumed, and everything went back to normal.

"Not likely!" Susan muttered, rummaging around in her bureau, restless and out-of-sorts. Two weeks had passed since they'd resumed work. During those two weeks, Susan spent too many of her waking hours forced to look into Jake's haunting eyes. Tormented at the sight of his smile. Enduring the lurid dimpling of his cheeks and the mellow seductiveness of his scent. Worst of all, she had to deal with his touch as he helped her over slippery rocks, or escorted her to dinner.

She wanted to scream at the man, *"Jake Merit, if you persist in acting gallant and attentive and witty, even for one more minute, I'll—I'll…"*

Sometimes it almost seemed as though he was slyly courting her. He was extremely courteous, though his touch was above reproach and his conversation without a shred of innuendo. She shook her head, throwing off the weird idea. Obviously her wayward fantasies were affecting her reasoning.

After that afternoon in the woods, when, for just a moment, she'd thought she saw—something—in his eyes, he'd been a perfect gentleman. Besides, she couldn't blame him for what happened. She'd been responsible. She'd even hit him! It was lucky for her he wasn't vindictive. He could have insisted Ed Sharp fire her. If a client like Jake Merit, worth hundreds of thousands of dollars in business, insisted she go, no matter how glowing her professional record might be, she would go.

"Ah!" She pulled her drawing pad out of the bottom dresser drawer. "I knew I brought you!" Snatching up her charcoals, she left the room. Work was over for the day, but there was still plenty of sunlight. Since Jake habitually retired to his office between five and seven o'clock to handle the daily details of work, she decided she'd take a solitary stroll, find some pleasant spot to sit and sketch. She enjoyed the peaceful solitude of her hobby. Sketching calmed her after a stressful day. And if she'd ever *needed* calming, she needed it now.

Her mind trailed back over the past two weeks. If it hadn't been for the fact that she kept running into pictures of Tatiana—on the living-room mantel as well as in the den adjoining Jake's bedroom, where Jake held their evening meetings—Susan might have allowed herself the pretty delusion that Jake was attracted to her.

"Get a grip," she mumbled, charging out of the mansion and across the back patio. "He runs his fingers down her face every time he gets near one of those photographs. That's not the action of a man attracted to *you!*"

He was merely a man with a painfully magnetic personality. He couldn't help being irresistible. It was a flaw he was born with and she would have to learn to deal with it. His looks, smiles and touches were nothing more nor less than his easygoing business manner. There was no point in reading more into it than that.

Clenching her hands, she marched away from the mansion—and from Jake—wishing the island was fifteen miles long instead of only five. She vowed she would find something interesting to draw, somewhere peaceful on Merit Island, and she would relax if it killed her.

As she moved off the manicured lawn, she headed

down a rocky path into a wooded valley, then upward to a cliff overlooking a curving finger of granite that jutted into the sea. She stilled, her heart leaping with surprise and anticipation. A man sat at the crest of the outcropping, fishing. An instant later, she realized the man wasn't Jake, but crotchety old King George.

She surveyed the elderly patriarch, with his rolled-up trouser-legs and bare feet. He wore a loose-fitting, colorful cotton shirt, unbuttoned and billowing over a white T-shirt. A crushed canvas hat, bedecked with fishing flies, was pulled low on his brow to avoid being stolen by the gusty breeze. A broken yellow feather, stuck in the brim, flapped wildly in the sea air.

He didn't look a thing like the bully she'd grown accustomed to. There was something nostalgic about the sight, even sweet. A hint of bleakness showed itself in the slump of his shoulders and the pensive stillness on his profile. For the first time since she'd met the old tyrant, Susan's heart went out to him. She'd never realized it before, but he was lonely. No wonder he yearned for grandchildren. She would bet a million dollars that he longed to teach them to fish and to play chess, to brighten up his solitary senior years.

Before she was conscious of what she was doing, she had taken a seat on the grassy slope and began to sketch. Time slipped away as she concentrated on her work. George hardly moved, so he couldn't be fly fishing. She decided he must have a cork or bobber in the water, and he waited and daydreamed, not caring if he got a bite or not. He just sat there, so still, gazing off into space.

She'd done several sketches before the one she now worked on. "Finally," she murmured. At last, she felt she'd captured the essence of the real George Merit—a man of fierce pride and poignant loneliness, with an unforeseen hint of whimsy in his soul. She smiled, gratified for the chance to have witnessed the old man like this. "You'll never annoy me quite as much after today," she murmured aloud. A tiny part of her even wished she could give him those grandchildren he craved.

She closed her eyes, squelching the daydream. "Susan," she warned, "I've told you about that! *Quit it!*"

"What have I done this time?"

She froze. Jake's voice was unmistakable. She made a face, hoping he'd been too far away to make out what she'd said. "Reel in your ego," she called, without turning. "Everything's not about you."

"What are you doing?" he asked.

She could hear his approach and shifted to glance over her shoulder. He wore the jeans and black knit shirt he'd worn all day. "I'm passing the time." Why was it that all he had to do was show up and her hard-earned calm scattered like quail flushed from high grass.

"Doing what?" He drew up beside her and knelt. His scent wafted around her and her discomfort level shot up a hundredfold.

It was too late to fling her drawing into the ocean, so she just sat there, stiff and unsettled. "Sketching." Her stomach fluttered. She hadn't meant for anybody to see her work. Especially Jake.

"Well, well..." he murmured.

She flicked him a worried look as he lifted his gaze to scan his father. Susan watched his profile as he glanced down at her sketch. "This is great, Susan." He lifted the artists' pad from her limp fingers. "You've captured a side of my father I'd almost forgotten existed." He faced her, and she was blown away by his eyes. In them, she saw sincerity and real appreciation.

"May I have this?" he asked.

She stared, her heart pounding in her ears. "What did you say?"

He took a seat beside her, settling her sketch pad on his thighs. "I asked if I could have this."

She'd heard him right after all. "You—you don't have to be nice, Jake." Her cheeks heated. "It's nothing. I sketch to relax, I..." She could feel a bout of babbling coming on. Embarrassed by his flattery, she reached for her pad.

"No, don't." He took her wrist. "I'm serious. It's wonderful."

His hand on her skin was gentle. "You don't give yourself enough credit." He indicated the drawing. "It would mean a great deal to me to have this."

He held her wrist, his eyes riveting. All she could manage was a brief, uneven nod.

He smiled and her pulse flew into orbit. "Thanks." He tugged on her arm. "Why don't I walk you back? It's nearly time for dinner."

Before she could decline, he had assisted her to her feet. She wasn't really surprised when he slid his hand along her arm to take her hand in his. She told herself to pull away. Yet somehow, she couldn't bring herself to tug free. Day by day, she continued to grow more emotionally frail, less able to withstand Jake's subtle sorcery.

He probably didn't realize what he was doing to her. Jake was a raging affliction and Susan was highly susceptible. Much more time around him and she would succumb to anything and everything he might suggest—even the briefest wordless gaze would have the power to fell her.

"What are you thinking about?" he asked. "You look so serious."

She jumped. "Oh—I..." What could she tell him?

Certainly not the truth. "I—I was just wondering how your family came to own a whole island full of emeralds."

He laughed. "We weren't a band of cutthroat pirates, if that's what you're thinking."

She glanced his way, fighting off her weakness for him. "I guess I haven't given it much thought."

His smile grew wry. "I'm flattered."

She looked away. "So—if you weren't pirates, and you didn't pillage and plunder to get it, how did your family come to own it?"

"I wish it was an exciting story," he said, his fingers entwined with hers, subtly sensual. "In a nutshell, just short of three hundred years ago, one of my ancestors gave King George II a prize stallion. The king was so taken with the animal, he gave my great-great-great-great-whatever-Maeret this island. It's been in the family ever since."

She glanced at him again, intrigued. "And which lucky Merit discovered emeralds?"

"According to family records, in the year 1890, Geoffery Merit, grizzled old fisherman and one lucky son of a—ahem—" he passed her a wink that curled her toes. "—fisherman, was digging a new well. And, as they say, the rest is history."

"So Geoffery gave up fishing to become a multizillionaire emerald mogul?" Susan asked, wishing she didn't feel so buoyant when he was near, so alive.

"It was a tough choice, but..." He motioned with the arm that held her art pad. "You don't see any fishing boats, do you?"

She glanced around, pretending to investigate. "Can't say that I do."

She had another thought and asked, "By the way, have

I been fitted with a tracking device? You seem to find me no matter where I am."

He laughed. "Nothing so clandestine. I just checked with security."

"Security?" She hadn't thought of that. "Oh my—heavens! Did they see us, uh, in the woods, when..." She experienced a rush of mortification. "We were—sparring?"

His grin disappeared. "Security cameras are placed around the shoreline to alert us to unauthorized vessels, Susan. Today, you were near enough to be caught on camera. Merit Island isn't a police state." He glanced away, looking toward the house. "I happened on you that day in the woods by chance." When he looked at her again, his exhale seemed as though it came from an unhappy man, and Susan was struck by the glimpse of vulnerability. "I hope you'll except my apology for—anything I might have done to provoke you."

Everything you do provokes me! she cried inwardly. *Especially your vulnerability!* Her heart reacting on its own, she smiled apologetically. "I'm the one who goaded you into sparring."

His lips curved vaguely. "And you punched me."

She experienced a well-deserved twinge of guilt, but shook her head, deciding to move the conversation to a lighter track. "I have no memory of that."

"You lie," he teased.

She peered at him from beneath her lashes. "Only when absolutely necessary."

He canted his head nearer, a lock of dark hair falling across his brow. "And under what circumstances do you find it absolutely necessary?"

His gaze lazily appraised her, quietly taunting. To her horror she could actually feel sexual magnetism radiate from him like death rays from Mars. What little resistance she still possessed was dying a grizzly death.

RENEE ROSZEL   103

felt quite easily appraised her unruly auntling. To her horror, she could actually feel sexual magnetism radiate from him that strong rays from Mars. While little resistance she still mustered was about to become a pretty dense

CHAPTER SEVEN

JAKE stood before the mantel in the mansion's living room. He stared at Tatiana's photograph for what seemed like forever. Finally, clamping his jaws, he solidified his decision. Lifting the frame, he whispered, "Don't make me feel guilty, Tati."

He ground out a curse, knowing the woman he'd loved and lost would never do that. Any guilt he felt was of his own making. Tati wouldn't have wanted him to suffer all these years. She would want him to find happiness.

He ran his fingers down her face, smiling sadly at the image he'd cherished for too many empty years. "All this torture has been my doing. I know that, now. It's my job to pull myself out of it." Turning the frame over, he lifted off the back. A moment later he'd slipped Susan's drawing of old King George in front of Tatiana's photograph.

Fighting off the stab of uncertainty, he replaced the frame on the mantel. After a difficult moment, he allowed himself to glance at the illustration. The whimsy Susan had lent to the artwork had its effect, and only seconds later he managed a real smile.

Susan was so unlike his quiet, regal mother and his saintly, sweet Tatiana. Susan was a what-you-see-is-what-you-get kind of woman. She said what she thought and did what she felt. She was forthright and sharp, willing and able to compete on a level playing field with any male. She had more guts than a lot of men he knew, yet she hadn't sacrificed her femininity.

He'd never thought freckles were particularly sexy, but he'd grown quite captivated by those damnable flecks chasing across her nose and scattering along her cheeks. He could tell her blush annoyed her. With an ironic quirk of his lips, he wondered if she had an inkling of how that crimson flush affected him *every blasted time?* Feelings he'd thought lost forever came roaring back, as distinct and potent as ever.

Never in his wildest dreams would he have thought her type would attract him. She was far from the demure women he'd always courted. Yet it was Susan and her pull-no-punches attitude about life who had helped him realize for the first time in over a decade that he wasn't simply a dead man walking. He was flesh and blood, and he'd wasted too much of his life wallowing in self-pity and survivor's guilt, just because he was alive.

He examined Susan's drawing and experienced a surge of exhilaration. He was fond of the freckle-faced, kick-boxing dynamo. Yes, Susan O'Conner—with her spunk, her big blue eyes and seductive blush—was his passage back to the land of the living. Though she couldn't re-place Tatiana in his heart, she was someone he could laugh with, make a family with. Those things were worth a great deal.

Regrettably, changing Susan's rabid no to his proposal into a yes would require great finesse. So far, his subtle courtship had made precious little progress. Each time he thought he sensed headway, he would catch her in a glance filled with misgivings. "I hope you have it in you, Merit, old buddy," he muttered. "Because, one false move, and you're toast."

"One week and five days," Susan mumbled as she entered the living room. "I just have to resist him for

one week and five days more! Then I'll be back in
Portland at my desk, safe and sound and out of tempta-
tion's clutches."

As dinner ended, Jake excused himself to take a business call and King George strutted off to bed, leaving
Susan with two unpalatable choices. She could go to bed
only to toss and turn, or she could walk off her restless-
ness. She decided to walk.

She recalled a lovely terrace outside the living room,
where the ocean breezes were soft and the scent of roses
from the garden was especially rejuvenating to sagging
spirits —and hopefully to eroding resolve. As she passed
through the elegant splendor of the room, her attention
was drawn to the exquisite Chagall above the mantel. She
paused in reverent appreciation for the artwork.

After a moment, as she took her first step away, a voice
in her head whispered. *There's something different about
that mantel.* She stopped and frowned, wondering what
her subconscious grasped that she hadn't. She turned
back. Though she didn't care to look at Tatiana's photograph, her attention moved there against her will. What
she saw stunned her.

The drawing of King George. Her drawing!

Seconds later, she found herself standing before the
fireplace, not sure she was seeing right. She lifted the
frame and stared. Jake had replaced the picture of his
precious Tatiana with the sketch of George? It hardly
seemed possible, but surely she could believe her own
eyes.

Puzzled, she replaced it, then retraced her steps toward
the terrace. Before she went outside, she turned back, her
heart doing an apprehensive lurch. She was sure she
would see Tatiana's face in the frame, certain she'd had
some crazy kind of hallucination.

No. The silver frame still held her artwork. She shook her head, baffled, but somewhere deep inside, scarcely willing to be acknowledged, a tiny part of her burst into tears of joy.

Walking outside, she moved to the terrace's stone railing and leaned against it. There was hardly any moon, but artful lighting in the gardens and along the house's perimeter gave her a striking view.

The evening air was cool, and Susan pulled her cardigan more securely around her. Inhaling the fragrant scent of roses, she worked to get her emotions under control. Jake's gesture, displaying her sketch, had brought her close to tears. She wondered at his use of Tatiana's frame, unable to decipher why he'd chosen that one. Doubtless, his father would never have allowed him to cover his mother's picture. Though she found it hard to imagine Jake doing that, either. But why Tatiana's?

He'd probably removed her photograph to a private shrine in his bedroom. She closed her eyes and swallowed hard. Even so, the acknowledgment of her artwork was kind of Jake. She couldn't remember ever being so touched.

The soft strains of music drifted from inside the house. Curious, she turned in time to see Jake come through the patio doors. He came to a halt when she turned. Backlit by the living-room brightness, his face was in shadow, but she sensed that he was smiling.

"Hi," he said, then strolled toward her, leaving the door ajar.

"Hi." *Must you always look so good?* she cried inwardly. He wore simple beige trousers and a dove-gray mock turtleneck. The sight drove her mad with longing— the way he walked and carried himself. The way the breeze toyed with his hair, cruelly trifling with her heart in the process.

His grin dimpled his cheeks and his eyes twinkled even in the dimness. With every step nearer, Susan's breathing became more and more labored. Working to rein in her emotions, she shifted to look away. "So—finished with your call?" She winced. *What a dumb question!*

"About fifteen minutes ago." He chose to stand in her direct line of vision, forcing her to look into his face. He lounged against the railing, watching her, his grin doing fiendish things to her heart. "I was afraid you'd gone to bed, but one of the servants said he saw you heading this way."

She chewed on her lower lip, inwardly cursing the vigilance of the household staff. "Did you want a meeting tonight? I'd thought we'd determined the—"

"No," he cut in softly, shifting to face her more directly. "No meeting. I thought we might talk."

She stared, unsure what to say. "Talk?" she finally said. "About what?"

He placed a hand on the rail. When his fingers grazed hers, she defensively slid away from his touch.

"Just talk, Susan," he said. "You may have heard of it." He canted his head toward her.

Susan felt an odd combination of emotions—trepidation mixed with expectancy. He'd been very attentive all day, though completely professional. But tonight there was something vaguely different in his manner. His aftershave coiling around her seemed to have an agenda that had nothing to do with the business of drilling for emeralds. She batted down the notion. A flirtatious *aftershave?* How idiotic! "Oh—*talk.* I think I've heard of that." Trying to keep her tone light, she added more tentatively, "Since you brought it up—you start."

He laughed, a marvelous, contagious sound. Unable to help herself, she smiled. "What's funny?"

He shook his head. "I changed my mind." Slipping her fingers into his, he drew her against him. "I feel like dancing."

She found herself breast to chest with him, swaying to the sensual strains of a popular song. She'd loved the tune from the first time she'd heard it. Now she was sorry it appealed to her. All she needed to be shoved over the edge was to have Jake hold her intimately, just like this, smile at her, just like this, with his coconspirator in crime a melody so blatantly contrived for lovemaking she felt the need to pound his chest and plead for mercy.

"I, er, don't really enjoy dancing," she croaked. It was a lie, but she sensed where Jake was concerned, a well-placed lie would be worth a thousand morning-after regrets.

His fingers splayed at her waist, drawing her closer to him. "Then why do you do it so well?" he asked, his lips grazing her temple.

She closed her eyes, commencing a count to ten in an attempt to hold on to her composure.

"I'll tell you what," he said, making her lose count. She began again. "Why don't you do to me what you did to old King George?"

She opened her eyes, giving up on her tally. Evidently, being snuggled in Jake's embrace wrecked her ability with numbers, and practically anything else that didn't deal directly with gazing into his eyes. *"What?"* She felt flustered, dazed. How did the man expect her to carry on any kind of conversation while he rubbed against her that way?

"The way you cured Dad about bothering you to play

chess," he explained. "Dance with me until I'm so humbled by your genius I'll never mention it again."

She peered up at him. With the reflected light from the garden his eyes seemed to glow. She'd never seen such an erotic sight, and her body reacted wildly, painfully. One more second of his intimate sexy-male-animal charm, and she didn't know what she might do, how she might disgrace herself. At her wit's end, she cried, "Why are you doing this?" Tears stung her eyes and her voice trembled. "Is life on the island so boring that embarrassing me is sport to you?"

He became instantly still. "Good Lord, no…"

Startled by the quiet shock in his voice, she blinked back tears, forcing herself to look directly into his eyes.

He watched her solemnly. The gentleness in his expression amazed her. "*Never*, Susan," he whispered. "I'd never want to embarrass you. I was trying…" He shook his head. "Is it so crazy that I might want to dance with you? That I might enjoy your company?"

She searched his face for signs of sarcasm. Naturally it was crazy to think…

Wait a minute, Susan, the reasoning portion of her brain counseled, *he said he enjoyed your company. That's all he said. Why is that so crazy? Just because it's Jake, you think he couldn't possibly enjoy your company? Are you such a loser that he can't simply want to dance with you?*

No, you certainly are not!

She straightened her shoulders and looked away for a second, telling herself to get a grip. She wouldn't think it was so crazy if some other man had taken her into his arms, suggesting they dance. She might not be Jake's beloved and perfect Tatiana, but she wasn't a troll he'd found under a bridge. Sucking in a breath, she looked up at him, at his handsome, solemn face. "I guess it's not crazy, Jake. I suppose, I—"

"Owe me one?"

She frowned, confused, a state he seemed to be able to keep her floundering in. "What?"

"I agreed to spar with you in the woods, so you're dancing with me," he said, his voice slightly husky. "That's what you were about to say, right?"

She cleared her throat, trying not to show how much she was affected by his heady nearness. Dancing with Jake was an utterly sensual experience. Any woman in her right mind would revel in it, not fight it! She tingled everywhere they touched, her passion for him sparked into flame, leaving her weak of body and will.

"Isn't that right?" he repeated in a dusky whisper.

With no desire to back out of his embrace, she gave in—at least a little—and nodded.

"Good," he whispered against her hair. When his lips grazed her brow, she had the most irrational impression that she'd been kissed.

The next few days were difficult for Susan. She found herself indulging in bizarre fantasies that she'd said yes to Jake when he'd proposed. Her nights passed in daffy self-indulgent dreams where she conjured up illusions of holding an infant in her arms, a tiny replica of Jake. The man she loved stood by her side, gazing at her with utter devotion.

When she wasn't asleep, she daydreamed of being held in his arms, of being made love to with tender kisses and sinfully sweet caresses. It was almost enough to drive her to playing chess with George, to keep her mind occupied, distance herself from Jake's emotional control.

His wit, his slyly seductive touch, his sexy smiles were

hard to resist. Yet it was his hushed, soulful looks that drove her to the brink of surrender. It was during those times she grew frantic, struggling to deny her longing and need.

He'd said nothing about love nor had he mentioned marriage again. His manner in her company, his quiet closeness, seemed completely professional, still her feminine antennae were up and receiving. No matter that he spoke to her only of cores and beryl, no one could convince her that Jake Merit wasn't transmitting strong signals of masculine interest.

But interest to do what? A sexual fling that would leave her vulnerable both emotionally and professionally. Susan found herself actually regretting her refusal of his marriage proposal more and more as each day passed. Though her decision had been right, she found herself wobbling. Wondering what she'd done. Questioning who she'd really hurt.

Jake was handsome, charming, a brilliant wit, and *sexy*. Hadn't she loved the man nearly half her life? She hated to think she'd made a huge mistake turning him down merely to salve her wounded pride. Neither of her previous fiancés had consumed her so completely with need as Jake did by the simple act of entering a room.

Heaving a despondent sigh, she rose from the easy chair before the bookcase in her bedroom. The dry biography she'd chosen to put her to sleep wasn't doing its job. She supposed it was more her fault than the book's. It was certainly dry enough reading.

Laying the volume in the chair, she checked the wall clock. Two-thirty. "Oh, fine, Susan," she muttered. "You have to get up in four-and-a-half hours. You'll look like a classic specimen of the red-eyed, lovesick nincompoop."

She caught a glance of herself in the mirror, at her tousled red-brown mane. Running her hands through the chaotic mass of hair, she only managed to muss it further. Tilting her head, she gave her reflection a seductive smirk, as though it was Jake staring back instead of her. "Come and get me, big boy." Her tone dripped with mock come-hither huskiness.

Turning on her heel, she grabbed her white terry robe and fumbled into a pair of matching scuffs. "I need—" She scowled as she knotted the sash, not sure how to verbalize what she needed "—to be very, very..." She clamped her jaws. Heading out her bedroom door, she gritted out, *"...somewhere else."*

Susan knew she'd lost her mind. That was okay, though. She needed to lose her mind. She needed to be relieved of any and all thinking processes. That was why she didn't bother to involve her brain as she tromped toward the woods. Her brain had been a huge impediment to her these past three weeks. No matter how she tried to keep herself on track, her thoughts kept veering toward torrid subjects that were out of bounds—just as Jake was.

Whatever he'd had on his mind these past weeks was wearing her down. If he wanted to sleep with her, why didn't he spit it out so she could slap his face and tell him to go straight to—to—well, he'd figure it out.

She had no intention of being seduced. Not that the idea hadn't burst into her mind a hundred times—one hundred examples of brain-betrayal. Silly fool that she was, she knew if she allowed herself to weaken, she would hold the memory of his kisses, his faithless caresses, in her heart, forever. But she would be ashamed of herself, of her weakness, and of him, for being less than the honorable man she believed him to be.

Maybe that was the worst of it. She didn't want Jake

to show himself unworthy of the pedestal she'd so carefully erected for him. She didn't want to be wrong about him. She wanted him, *but she didn't want him to want her.* At least, not for only one night.

She laughed contemptuously as she made her way through the trees and down a rocky path. She loved Jake Merit, and she knew he could never love her. She would give anything if he would step down from his pedestal so she could get on with her life. Yet she didn't want him stepping down by showing himself to be a womanizer. Ironically it would solve all her problems. They could have their fling, and she could get over him.

Knowing Jake fully and completely was what she craved most. Still, she couldn't bear the thought of watching his fall, or of being an active partner in it.

Would she rather suffer, never knowing the joy of his kisses, only to be reassured that he deserved her unrequited devotion? Did that make any sense at all? *Not a crumb!* "Susan you have definitely gone 'round the bend!"

She came to a halt on a bluff, noticing she was in the spot where she'd sketched Old King George on the rocky peninsula. Still unwilling to think, she headed down the slope to where the granite finger curled out into the sea. It looked like a good place to sit and—*not* think.

Her eyes had adjusted enough so she had no difficulty seeing. Clambering over the uneven surface, she faced the fact that her scuffs weren't the best choice in footwear, though they were better than nothing on the cold stone. To reach the big, flat rock where George had sat, she edged around a ridge, keeping one hand on the boulders that led to the sitting rock, as she'd come to think of it.

She was within a couple of feet of her objective when

a loose pebble made her skid sideways. Caught off guard, she jerked to right herself, overcompensating. Suddenly she was airborne, falling backward. Her arms outstretched, flapping in a futile attempt to take flight, she plunged into the churning tide.

She went under, but surfaced quickly. Her main trouble was her robe. Soaked with seawater, it felt like a thousand-pound weight. She yanked the sash open and shrugged out of it as she paddled toward shore. Her slippers were history, though she could see one when it popped up. She ignored it. The water was icy and she needed to get out, fast. Saving one slipper wasn't worth the risk.

Gurgling and snorting seawater, she battering through the surf toward the jagged outcropping. She found her leg movement restricted, making kicking difficult. Her drawstring pajama bottoms had come loose and her waistband rode around her knees. With a couple of freeing flails, they were no longer her problem. Along with her robe and slippers, her pants had become the property of Poseidon.

Coughing and sputtering in the churning water, she grabbed for the slippery rock. Her first two attempts failed, but at last, chilled to the bone, she stubbed her toe on something solid. Groaning with pain, but grateful she still had feeling in her feet, she hooked her toes over a lip of stone, then managed to snatch a jutting shelf of granite above the water's surface. Her fingers were frigid and her body jerked with tremors, but she managed to hold on.

Muttering about how idiotic she was to have placed herself in such a precarious position, she began to struggle upward, fearful that the wild shaking of her body would wrench her loose, and she'd sink into the sea, never to be seen again. Maybe using her brain would have been a good idea, even if it had just been for a few seconds before she'd decided to make this foolhardy trek onto wet rock in the middle of a black night.

Something warm caught her around the wrist, and she snapped her head up to see what had seized her. Though her eyes stung with saltwater, there was no mistaking the blurry image before her. Jake knelt on the sitting rock, his features marred with worry. He'd extended one arm down over the edge and grasped her by the wrist.

She gasped, then was sorry, since it allowed her to inhale the briny liquid dripping from the hair. "Jake?" she croaked.

He towed her the rest of the way up. Once hefted to the rock, Susan sank to her knees, her body quaking too badly to support her. Jake smoothed her hair out of her eyes, his fingers hot and gentle. "You're freezing," he murmured. "You need to get out of that soaked shirt."

Her body convulsed as her muscles struggled to create warmth. When she felt his fingers grazing her breasts as he unbuttoned her pajama top she grasped what he'd said and became aware of what he was doing. Instinctively she slapped his hand away. "What—d-do y-y-you t-t-t..."

"Shut up," he muttered. "You can be modest later." With a growl of frustration he ripped the thing off and tossed it aside. The night was black, and she could barely see his face, but she sensed his eyes on her. Sensed his gaze raking over her. "Lord..." he whispered.

With quaking limbs she made a feeble attempt to cover herself. "Don't..." she whimpered, embarrassed.

The fragile plea had its effect, for almost immediately something engulfed her. She felt Jake's hand against her face as he stroked sopping hair behind her ear. "Can you stand?'' he asked softly, warm fingers lingering at her temple.

Still violently trembling, she drew away from his touch and nodded. Pushing up on wobbly legs, she hauled the blanket, or whatever it was Jake had covered her with, as close to her body as she could. When she took a step, something made her trip.

''Damn.'' Jake caught her against him, wrapping her in the heavenly warmth of his embrace. ''It's the fringe,'' he murmured near her ear.

She peered at his face, her senses numb. She had a sinking feeling it would be best if they stayed that way. ''F-f-fringe?''

He frowned. ''It was the first thing I could grab.'' Before he went on, he lifted her into his arms. ''I didn't have much time.''

She sucked in a breath as he drew her close and began to make his way toward solid ground. She stared longingly at his profile, fighting the need to put her arms around his neck and lay her head on his shoulder.

Her shivering eased somewhat. Deciding she needed to get her mind on something besides her need for Jake, she glanced down at herself. Whatever he'd wrapped her in was warm, but it wasn't a blanket. ''What is this?''

''A wall-hanging.'' Jake jumped off the rock onto the pebble-strewn shore.

She was amazed. ''A wall-h-hanging? I'm wearing a wall-hanging?''

He didn't smile, but there was definite easing in the severity of his expression. ''It could have been worse. At least the one I yanked off the wall is silk.''

She eyed him fretfully, afraid she was thawing enough to start to understand the true extent of her humiliation. ''Uh, how did you h-happen to be out here with a silk wall-hanging at two-thirty in the morning?'' She prayed it was some kind of weird ritual the inordinately wealthy carried out every year—something to do with the approach of autumn and third-quarter stock dividends.

He shifted his attention from the path that lead up the slope to the woods, and looked at her. ''Do you want the whole truth or the watered-down-to-keep-you-from-committing-suicide version?''

She winced. ''The second one. I'm not up to suicide right now.''

His lips curved vaguely, but she didn't think it was with amusement. More likely it was—on second thought, he *was* laughing at her. Susan O'Connor, the clumsy, naked night-prowler, wrapped in a wall hanging, who couldn't stomach the whole humbling truth.

''Okay,'' he began. ''I was asleep when I got a call from security—''

''*Security!*'' She'd forgotten about those dratted shore-line cameras. ''Blabbermouths!''

He eyed her for a flash, then focused on the path. ''That's what they get paid for, Susan. Anyway, they notified me you were out here just as you fell in. They thought it would be less embarrassing for you if I came and got you.''

''They thought having you come out here and rip off the only clothes I had left would be less embarrassing than *what,* I'd like to know?''

''Less than having several armed, uniformed men do it.'' He captured her gaze and held it. ''And the blanket wouldn't have been silk.''

They stared at each other for a minute. Susan had to admit, if only to herself, there was the tiniest possibility the other scenario would have been more embarrassing.

She wondered what the unwatered-down story sounded like.

Jake stopped walking and searched her face. The hint of a worried frown rode his brow. "What in blazes were you doing?" he asked quietly. "What were you thinking, Susan?"

She felt like the worst kind of fool. Unable to hold eye contact, she looked away and shrugged. "I wasn't thinking," she said at last, through a long sigh. "I'd had enough of thinking. I didn't want to think. I wanted to—to…" She shook her head.

Freeing a hand from her silken cocoon, she brushed back a soggy wisp of hair. "I don't know," she admitted, flicking him a solemn glance. "It's complicated."

"Some people think I'm kind of bright," he offered. "Maybe I could help."

The night breeze played with his hair. Susan's gaze roamed over his wonderful face as he watched her. *Yes, you could help, Jake,* her mind threw out forlornly. *You're the only person on earth who can. Just tell me you love me and everything will be fine.* She chased away the foolishness and shook her head. "I don't—think so. But thanks."

His lips twisted ruefully. "I should be getting used to your rejections by now."

Muscle flexed in his cheeks and she sensed he was annoyed. Could she really blame him? He'd had to leave a warm bed to rescue her from her own stupidity, and she wouldn't even give him a hint as to why. "You're a client, Jake, not a psychologist," she said. "And please don't tell me it's just one of the services you offer. I've caused you enough inconvenience for one night."

After a brief tension-filled pause, he nodded, but she noticed the slight flare of his nostrils. He was aggravated, and she hated that. But there was no help for it. Nothing on the planet would drag the truth out of her. Besides, Jake would be the last person who would want to hear this particular truth.

As he walked, her gaze traveled down along his square jaw, then to his throat. Tendons of strain were visible in the dimness. For the first time, she realized he wore no shirt.

Before she was aware that she was going to, she peeked down. He had on a pair of dark shorts.

"What did you expect?" he asked.

Her gaze rocketed to his. "Expect?"

"Were you afraid I'd be naked?"

Her cheeks flushed, and for once she was glad, since moments ago she's been so cold she didn't think she had any warm blood left in her veins. "I—I didn't—I never—the thought never occurred to me!" She wasn't absolutely convinced that was true, but she didn't intend to tell him.

A brow rose, clearly indicating his doubt. "Should I apologize for wasting time putting on shorts?"

He slept in the nude? The image that leaped in her brain further heated her face. "As far as I'm concerned, it was time well spent," she retorted, more upset with herself than with him. Whether he wore—or didn't wear—clothes to bed was none of her business. "And while we're on the subject of sleeping attire," she blurted, "I don't think it was necessary for you to rip off my pajama shirt." She bit her lip, sorry she'd brought it up. Her face was fiery now. So much for her fear of freezing. She fairly burned with humiliation.

Halting, he snagged her gaze. "If it makes you feel any better, it was too dark to see—much."

"That doesn't sound like an apology."

He didn't flinch at her rebuke as she expected he would. His eyes never left hers. She noted a subtle change in his features, but it didn't look like remorse. "I'm sorry it was too dark to see much," he whispered.

Her mouth dropped open in shock. "Excuse me?"

"Would you rather I lie?" he asked, his expression solemn.

"Yes!" she cried. She wanted to be outraged, but a part of her was thrilled. *A stupid part,* she berated inwardly. "Look, Jake..." She squirmed in his arms, suddenly needing to put distance between them before she did something she'd regret for the rest of her days. "Put me down. I appreciate what you did, but I can make it from here on my own."

His jaws worked again and he glanced away for a second before making eye contact. "I know you can make it on your own, Susan," he said quietly. "But I can't." His tone low and husky, he added, "Not anymore."

She watched him warily, perplexed. In the past few minutes he'd said some strange and disconcerting things. What, exactly, was going on?

With a melancholy smile, he lowered her to her feet, then with gentle hands turned her to face him. For a moment he watched her face. With extraordinary gentleness, he tugged the silk fabric more snugly around her, brushing her throat with his knuckles. Thrill after thrill of yearning sang through her body with the brief, erotic brush of his hands. When his gaze came back to rest on her questioning eyes, he merely stared for a long moment.

She stared back, baffled about what might be going through his head. "Jake?" she asked at last. "Tell me."

One corner of his mouth lifted, his expression oddly wistful. "Marry me, Susan." He took her hand and lifted her fingertips to his lips, grazing them with a kiss. "You make me smile—deep down. I haven't felt that way in years. For that incredible gift, I'll do my best to make you happy. I'll never lie to you. I'll give you a home, children and my fidelity. You do want a home—and children…" He lifted his gaze from her hand to meet hers. "Don't you?"

Stunned by his murmured pledge, Susan could only stand there, mute. Her fingers tingled where he'd kissed them. She hadn't expected this—not after her testy refusal. An offer for a quick tumble, yes, but not this. Not marriage!

Jake lowered her hand, and smoothed the hanging over her shoulders, his warm hands taking a slow, sensuous slide along her arms, stilling just above her elbows. "You don't have to answer now," he said with an encouraging smile. "But please do me the honor of thinking about it." Gently he squeezed her arms, as if to assure her of the earnestness of his vow. "Okay?"

She couldn't move, couldn't speak.

He looked away and she watched him strive to refresh his smile before he turned back. The awareness of how hard he was trying to move on with his life, and how difficult her continued silence was for him, brought tears to her eyes. "I know you didn't expect to be proposed to while sopping wet and wrapped in old dry goods." He shook his head and she glimpsed real distress cross his features. "I should have waited—should have thought of a romantic way to do this."

She swallowed, her throat dry as grit. She didn't need romance, she needed Jake! But did she dare believe a marriage built on anything less than mutual, profound love could really work?

He indicated the mansion in the distance. "I'll walk with you."

"No." The sound of her own voice in the stillness startled her and she blinked.

He inclined his head, his brows knitting. "You don't want me to walk with you?"

She shook her head. "No—I mean, that's okay. Fine." What had she said no about? Was her last shred of sanity answering the question she'd asked herself—whether such a union would work, when all the passion was so tragically one-sided?

He bent closer. "What was the no for, then?" She watched as he visibly swallowed, and her heart melted at the show of vulnerability. Jake Merit truly meant this proposal. He'd thought about it and for whatever crazy, wonderful reason, he was actually making a commitment.

To her!

She shook her head in disbelief.

"No?" he repeated, sounding discouraged.

She looked up, lost in a daze of disbelief and wonder.

"Won't you even think about it?" Dark, earnest eyes probed hers. "Can't you give the idea a little time?"

He hadn't mentioned love. He didn't love her. Tatiana still filled his heart. That part of the offer hadn't changed. But this time, she sensed he genuinely wanted to move forward, reenter the land of the living. *Susan, Susan,* her thawing brain cried, *Don't weaken! Remember why you said no in the first place! Remember—Oh, shut up! I love this man! I've loved him too long and too hard to turn him down a second time!*

She faced the truth. She had no choice. Jake Merit was her one, true love. Whether she held his heart or not, he had held hers for years. She would consent to be his wife and she would gladly, joyously give him the children he wanted—they both wanted. Her tears overflowed as she made a silent vow to save him with her devotion. Her love for him would be enough. "I don't need to give it any more thought, Jake," she whispered.

Two deep lines of distress appeared between his eyes, and he looked away. "I understand."

Lifting her hands to his cheeks, she drew him back to face her. "No, you don't."

CHAPTER EIGHT

JAKE WAS surprised when Susan's fingers coaxed him to face her. He wasn't accustomed to losing, but on those few occasions when he did, he took the loss with more aplomb than he exhibited now. Feeling gut-punched, he met her gaze.

The night was drawn around them like a black cloak, but he had no difficulty making out her features. He couldn't see her freckles or tell if she was blushing, but he was surprised to discover that she was smiling, and her eyes glistened with tears. She blinked and a silvery drop slid down her cheek. He frowned, confused.

"My answer is yes, Jake," she whispered. "I will marry you."

An odd, controlled excitement filled his body, as though he couldn't quite trust his hearing. He supposed he could believe her smile, but her tears?

"You will?" He searched her face, not believing his good luck. Another tear trailed after the first and his gut clenched. She had accepted, but it wasn't the fairy tale, head-over-heels experience she'd dreamed of. Women had certain expectations about marriage proposals. They wanted moonlight and tender words. *Damn!* Because of his rash, heavy-handed charge into the thick of it, he'd granted her neither. His smile was half grimace. "Are you sure this is what you want?"

She nodded. "I'll give you a family, Jake. I love children." She swallowed, lowering her eyes. "And I'll do my best to make you happy."

When she met his gaze again, he felt a curious, tingling shock. A sudden urgency he couldn't explain came over him and he took her into his arms, leaning down to kiss her.

Rather than present him with her lips as he'd expected, he was met with her cheek. At the last instant, she'd turned her head. He hesitated, but only for a second before he pressed his lips against her cheek.

A twinge of disappointment pricked him. Plainly this was all too new, too artificial, for her to deal with yet. She'd said she would give him the family he wanted, so she'd accepted that their marriage would be the customary kind, with all the physical ramifications that birthing babies required. She merely needed a little time to get used to the idea. After all, ten minutes ago, she had no more inkling he was about to ask her to marry him than she'd had that he would appear out of the darkness and haul her from the sea. To be honest, the idea to propose, then and there, hadn't been the way he'd planned it, either.

Holding her close, he allowed himself a brief, if melancholy, smile, then he tenderly kissed the top of her head. "Don't worry, Susan," he murmured. "This is right." He backed away, smoothing back her hair. "I feel it." Trailing his thumb across her fiery cheek, he wiped away a tear. Hesitantly, and with no desire to do so, he released her. "I'd better get you back." Noticing that the fabric that draped her body had slipped off one shoulder, he tugged it up, brushing softly rounded flesh. His reaction was unexpected and powerfully sensual. "We have a—" The words came out sounding like a rusty gate and he cleared his throat. "We have a full day of drilling ahead of us, Susan. We both need sleep."

He draped a supportive arm around her. "Be careful

of the fringe," he said, taking singular note of her scent. Even mixed with seawater and the muskiness of the silk hanging, he could detect the fragrance that was so uniquely Susan, and it heated his blood. He was amazed and grateful she made him feel—well *feel,* period. He'd never expected to experience again anything close to the way he'd felt about—

"When?" she asked, drawing his puzzled glance.

He leaned closer, for her question had been almost too faint to hear. "When what?"

She bit her lower lip, her glance brief and tentative. "When do you see this marriage taking place?"

He felt like a dolt. Only a moment ago, he'd asked her to marry him. Just because she'd said yes didn't mean everything was settled. He needed to get his mind off the way she felt and smelled! She might have said yes, but considering the cheek kiss, it was clear she wasn't hampered by awkward sensual distractions. He smiled an apology. "Soon, I hope."

She looked away. "Friday is my last day."

"Would Saturday work for you?"

Without glancing at him, she nodded.

At breakfast the next day, Jake and Susan broke the news to old King George. It seemed like only five minutes later every servant and miner could be seen whispering behind their hands and wagging their eyebrows.

Susan called her mother and father, retired and living in Florida, and her sister, Yvette, who lived in Kansas with her husband and three small children. That was pretty much her guest list except for her boss, Ed Sharp, and a few friends in Portland.

She went about her work surrounded by a lot of bustle

and brouhaha. It was the weirdest and most exhausting week in her life, with drilling, examining and compiling core-hole samples, *plus* planning a wedding.

The ceremony would be intimate, held in the mansion's living room. Jake flew in a designer friend from New York to help Susan with her dress. She spent several nights imprisoned with the older woman as her simple, yet elegant wedding frock was created from a few luscious yards of handwoven, ivory charmeuse and antique French lace.

Susan had to give Jake credit: when he wanted a wedding, he got a wedding—with all the trimmings. She spent most of her limited wedding-planning time merely nodding her approval, amazed by the splendor that an excess of money could produce. For as few guests as would be in attendance, a twelve-tiered cake that could feed a third-world country, seemed excessive. But the twittering, bustling wedding professionals who suddenly appeared to handle everything, were good at what they did and seemed genuinely desirous to please. Susan found very little to complain about.

Well—except when it came to Jake. Oh, there was no complaining about the man. He was attentive, charming, even dear at times, listening when she had questions or concerns about the wedding spiraling out of control. With an indulgent smile he assured her that she had the ultimate say. Anything she didn't like, or wanted changed, she only had to express, and it would be done.

She hadn't needed to test his assurance more than once or twice, but that was enough to discover her word was law. Susan's first inkling of what being the wife of Jake Merit would mean became clear when whole rooms of people came to respectful attention when she walked in. Without hesitation they dropped whatever they were doing and scurried to do her bidding. This newly acquired authority, as Jake's betrothed, was so absolute it was almost frightening.

Hectic days of work, collating a mountain of data, combined with the frantic pace of wedding preparations, rocketed Susan through Wednesday, Thursday and Friday. Several times she'd tried to tell Jake about Yvette, and that they'd met before. She knew the instant he saw her, he would remember. But they never seemed to have a moment alone. She didn't know if that fact was Jake's doing or merely the chaotic circumstances. She prayed it was the latter, but with every passing hour, she found herself weighed down more heavily with one aching regret—that she didn't hold absolute dominion over Jake's heart.

Saturday dawned with Susan in a dazed state of unreality. Today, September 1st, was her wedding day. In mere hours she would marry Jake Merit, the man of her dreams. She stretched and started to sit up, but as she came fully awake depression washed over her and she sank back to stare at the ceiling. This should be the happiest day of her life, yet unrelenting misery plagued her.

"I love you, Jake," she murmured, wishing their relationship was such that she could say it to him. They hadn't even kissed. Of course, that was entirely her fault. He'd tried to kiss her to seal their engagement, but at the last second she'd panicked and turned away, unable to bear his mercy kisses.

She would have to change her tune about that, and fast. Mercy kisses or no, she'd pledged herself to him, and that meant accepting whatever crumbs of affection he offered her, however mechanical or passionless the act. Within hours she would be his wife, and she had promised him children.

She heaved a sigh, thinking back about the way he'd suggested today as their wedding day. *Would Saturday work for you?* Even in her emotional tumult, she'd almost snapped, "I'll pencil it in, Mr. Merit," but she'd resisted the urge. How many times had she reminded herself that nobody's life was perfect. With his sincere proposal, she'd been given more than she'd ever dared hope. How much could one missing heart mean to her?

"Everything…" she cried softly.

A tear slid from the corner of her eye, skimming across her temple.

"Knock, knock?"

The sound of a familiar female voice, and a light rapping on the door brought Susan bolt upright. "Yvette?" Embarrassed for her bout of self-pity, she wiped the moisture from her face.

"Yes, and Mom's here, too. You decent, Susu?"

"Barely." She threw back the covers and jumped out of bed. "Come on in!"

The door opened as Susan dashed to greet them. "Mom!" She hugged Ida Jean O'Conner with all her strength then turned toward her older sister as she closed the door. "Vetie!"

"Brat!" Yvette gave her sister an admonishing pat on the rump. "Keeping secrets from your big sister about snagging the most eligible bachelor in Maine! *Shame on you!*"

The sisters embraced and exchanged cheek kisses. "Now, I want *every* juicy detail!"

Heat flooded Susan's face. If Yvette knew how pitifully devoid of juiciness the details were, she'd be shocked.

"Vetie," Ida Jean scolded in her quiet way, "don't

pester your sister about things that are none of your business.''

Susan backed out of Yvette's hug, glanced at her mother, then broke eye contact. Self-conscious, she smoothed down the oversize T-shirt she'd slept in since her involuntary dip in the ocean. "You're early, aren't you?" she asked, needing a change of subject. "Where's Dad?''

"Oh, he's checking out our rooms," Yvette said. "Counting the towels, inspecting the soap. You know how Dad is."

Susan grinned at the reminder. Chester O'Conner had always been a difficult traveler. "I have a feeling the Merit mansion's accommodations will stand up, even under Daddy's fussy scrutiny."

"If it doesn't, I hope you realize the wedding's off," Yvette joked. "Remember the fit he threw when he realized my Frankie didn't flatten and roll his toothpaste tube from the bottom?" She pantomimed being strangled.

Susan joined her sister in laughter.

"Now girls..." Ida Jean took their hands and lead them further into the room. "We have things to do. Leave your poor father alone."

"We're not bothering him, Mom," Yvette said through a giggle. "We're just—"

"I know what you're *just*," Ida Jean interrupted with a motherly shake of her perfectly coiffed head. "Your father is a brilliant man with high standards. Which, I might add, would not include this conversation." Turning to Susan, she smiled. "What can your sister and I do to help you get ready, dear?"

"Oh!" Yvette snapped her fingers. "Before I forget, Jake gave me a message for you, Susu."

Apprehension skittered along Susan's spine as she peered at her sister. "You—you saw him?"

She planted her hands on slim hips. "Of course! He met the boat." She sighed theatrically. "He's every bit as gorgeous as when I last saw him." Wistfully she shook her head. "I didn't know it then, but he'd already met that Tatiana woman while visiting France earlier that December, during Harvard's Christmas break." As Yvette chattered on, oblivious, Susan pulled in a long breath to get her emotions under control. She'd tried so hard to forget Tatiana. But now it seemed her own family conspired against her with painful reminders.

"The few times he took me out to holiday parties, he just needed a date." Yvette shrugged. "He'd already fallen for Tatiana, so I was only somebody to have on his arm. He was *terribly* charming, but I could tell our relationship wasn't going anyplace. Anyway, dating Jake definitely boosted my ego for those few..." Her glance drifted to Susan's face, and her animated features instantly sobered. "Oh..." Reaching out, she squeezed Susan's arm. It wasn't until then that she realized her face must have registered pain at the reminder of Jake's lost love.

"Gee, Susu, I didn't mean to—what I mean is—Tatiana's in the past. *Way* in the past!" Yvette's grin flickered back on. "Jake's marrying *you,* today."

Susan worked on her smile. "What—what's the message?"

Yvette's brow furrowed. "What message?"

Susan shook her head at her sister. She was a lovely, fragile-looking blonde without a freckle marring her pretty face, the image of their mother. Susan, on the other hand, stood several inches taller than both women, and sported her dad's auburn hair and freckles. Susan had never thought about it before, but Yvette possessed a delicate beauty, not unlike Tatiana. "Vetie," she reminded quietly, "you said Jake sent me a message."

"Oh, right." She giggled. "Silly me. He said to tell you he remembers who used to call him a Pushy Jughead." Her fine brows dipped. "He seemed surprised to see me. Didn't he know you and I are sisters?"

Susan closed her eyes and shook her head. "He does now." She faced Yvette again. "Anything else?" As far as the wedding was concerned, she didn't think the fact that she'd sassed him at fifteen would be a deal-breaker, but...

Yvette shook her head. "No—oh, yes." She grinned devilishly. "He said, 'Tell Susan we have a date at four o'clock. She has a tendency to forget to get married." Yvette poked her sister in the ribs. "I guess you told him a few things, huh? He didn't seem too terrified that you'd run away from *him*." She winked, leaning conspiratorially close. "Should I hazard a guess why?"

Susan's face blazed at the insinuation that she and Jake were lovers.

"*Vetie!*" Ida Jean rebuked. "You're incorrigible. Look at Susu. Her face is as red as a tomato!" Ida Jean placed an arm around her younger daughter and led her away from Yvette. "You get dressed, dear. Jake said he'd have breakfast sent up. Yvette and I are here to do whatever you need. We'll be settling into a suite in the north wing."

"Oh?" Susan experienced a surge of hope. "Are you staying for a visit?"

Ida Jean waved off the idea. "No, dear. The room is just ours to rest in and for changing clothes." She patted Susan's cheek. "Besides, after the wedding, you and Jake will be honeymooning. You don't want your parents and sister hanging around.''

Visions of Jake and her doing—well—*honeymoon things* flashed into her mind's eye. Did she dare hope their honeymoon would be the stuff fantasies were made of? Awkwardly she cleared her throat. ''We—we're not going anywhere.''

Ida Jean laughed. ''Well—nevertheless. This evening, your father and I are flying to Wichita with Yvette, to see our granddaughters. I know they've grown like weeds since Christmas.'' She puckered her lips as though in thought. ''Now, where was I? Oh, yes, I was about to say, after you eat, when you're ready for us, telephone our suite. Hmm?''

Susan nodded, ''Okay, Mom.''

''By the way, Jake said he'd be off the island for several hours. It'll be safe for you to join us and Jake's charming father for lunch, with no danger of seeing your groom.''

Susan looked at her mother. ''Jake will be gone?'' The news about George being charming flitting in and out of her brain. ''Why? What's he doing?''

Yvette tittered. ''He's not running away, if that's what you're worried about. He's picking up the ring.'' She narrowed her eyes, her expression mischievous. ''I can't wait to see the boulder he slips on your finger, Susu.'' She wagged her own unpretentious wedding set in the air, giving it a grudging once-over. ''I may be forced to die of jealousy.''

Wishing she felt less despondent, Susan smiled at her sister's clowning. Yvette was kidding. She and her husband, Frank Moore, a major in the Air Force, were a match made in heaven. Yvette would have worn a piece of twisted wire as a wedding ring, as long as Frank had given it to her. She inhaled a shaky breath, fighting off a surge of envy.

So, Jake planned to pick up her wedding ring? That momentous news made little impact. She didn't care if it was the most magnificent ring in the world, it would be a poor substitute for what she really craved from Jake.

If he only knew—or cared—that one adoring glance from him would mean the world to her.

"You wanted to see me, Dad?" Jake paused at the door of his father's den. All dark wood and leather, the place reminded him of one of those starched turn-of-the-century Englishmen's clubs. The room seemed even darker because of the acres of beet-red velvet curtains, always drawn, giving the room a bloody cast.

The old tyrant stood with his back to Jake, removing something from a wall safe the size of a closet. After spinning the tumblers to lock it, he turned. Clad in a plum-colored brocade smoking jacket over a crisp white ruffled shirt and tuxedo pants, he beamed at his son. "My boy," he roared, holding out a large green velvet box. "Do you remember this?"

Jake nodded. "Mother's jewels."

George walked to his ornate desk where a hand-carved jade chess set dominated. Laying the case down with a reverence Jake hadn't seen in his father's behavior since his mother's death, the older man opened the lid. He motioned to Jake. "Come here, boy."

Skeptical, Jake pushed away from the doorjamb and approached his father, wondering at his jovial mood. "I don't have much time, Dad. I have to leave for the mainland in a few minutes."

"This won't take long." George lifted out a dainty tiara of diamonds and emeralds. "I think your mother would have wanted Susan to wear this.'' He held it up so Jake could admire it in the light. "My beloved Rebecca wore it on our wedding day. What do you think?''

Jake's glance moved from the exquisite headpiece to his father's face as he turned the object in his hands, admiring the sparkle and twinkle of the jewels. His features had softened and Jake sensed he'd called to mind his own wedding.

"It's very pretty," Jake said, drawing his father's gaze.

"I'd like to give it to Susan, if you think she'd accept it.''

Jake's lips quirked in an ironic smile. It seemed he wasn't the only Merit who could tell Susan hadn't taken Jake up on his offer of marriage for money and position. Evidently George sensed she'd made an earnest commitment to be Jake's wife and the mother of his children.

After a minute, Jake shrugged.

"If she won't accept it, tell her it's tradition in the Merit family for brides to wear it. I think she'll take it on that basis, at least for today.''

Feeling closer to his father than he had in years, Jake smiled. "Thanks.''

George blustered, his customary scowl returning. "You two had better give me a grandbaby by next year at this time.''

Jake shook his head. "Way to go, Dad. For a minute, I thought you were actually being unselfish.'' Turning on his heel, he headed for the exit.

The hours disappeared in a whirlwind of activity. Susan could hardly remember most of the morning and not much more of the afternoon. As she dressed for the wedding, Yvette chatted while her mother bustled around with last-minute details, making sure Susan had something old, new, borrowed and blue.

The borrowed part had been accomplished by George, stunning everybody when he'd presented Susan with a tiara, modest in size, but breathtaking in subtle elegance. Yvette slipped it on Susan's head, declaring how perfect it looked surrounding the artful mass of auburn hair she'd arranged for her sister's wedding.

Chester O'Conner finally made an appearance and gave Susan a stiff hug and a peck on the cheek. It seemed he hadn't been able to find a thing wrong with their suite. Even the blooming plants on the grounds matched the interior decor.

Moments after Chester's arrival, Susan was summoned from her room. The wedding was about to begin. In a state of nervous euphoria, she allowed Yvette and her father to escort her down the stairs. Nothing seemed real. Could she really be about to *marry* Jake?

As a tuxedo-clad pianist played Mozart on the grand piano near the back of the living room, Yvette stepped beyond the double-doored entry to begin the processional as matron of honor and Susan's only bridesmaid.

Chester O'Conner looked elegant, if a bit fidgety in his tuxedo, as he stood beside his youngest daughter. Susan had only seen him in a tuxedo one other time, seven years ago when he gave Yvette away.

He seemed to sense her perusal and turned. With an awkward smile, he patted the hand that held his arm.

Though she clutched a small bouquet of white roses and baby's breath, she reached over to squeeze his fingers. "I'm okay, Daddy," she murmured. "Are you?"

She watched his Adams apple bob. "I don't know why

it is," he said, "but weddings get me more keyed up
than a championship chess match."

She knew what he meant. Though she smiled to re-
assure him, she felt as if she'd been lashed to a pole in
front of a firing squad.

No! Susan! she scolded silently. *Don't do this to yourself! You can make it work. Just because you're going
into this marriage the only one in love, don't torture
yourself by thinking you'll end up making him regret his
decision.*

The wedding march began and Susan jerked as though
coming awake. Self-consciously, she met her father's
questioning gaze. "I'm fine." Summoning every ounce
of courage she possessed, she smiled.

"Then I think we'd better go," he said.

She nodded, tried to swallow, but her throat was
blocked with emotion.

Chester placed his hand on the fingers gripping his
arm, then walked with her around the corner into the
wide entrance. The room was awash in late-afternoon
sunshine, tasteful antiques and accessories serving as a
graceful backdrop. Colorful bouquets abounded. The
guests sat in ivory brocade-covered folding chairs, situ-
ated on either side of an aisle. As Susan and her father
entered, those in attendance rose as one, and turned.

She sought out Jake, and her breath caught. He stood
before the marble hearth, his back to her, so tall and
handsome, clad in classic black. He clenched and unclenched one fist. Plainly the decision to move on with
his life was giving Jake an emotional pounding.

Panic washed over Susan, and she had to fight to keep
from being overwhelmed by a sinking despair. If she
hadn't been clinging to her father, she would have sagged
to the floor. With an effort she held her head high, hoping

he suffered from normal bridegroom jitters, that his resolve to leave the past where it belonged would win the day.

Please, Jake... she cried inwardly, blinking back forlorn tears. *Look at me!*

CHAPTER NINE

JAKE KNEW this marriage was his chance to grow whole again. He knew Tatiana was gone, and Susan was on her way down the aisle. For an instant his determination faltered, unsettling him. With an unspoken curse, he imposed steely control over himself. This union was right. He felt it with more certainty than he'd felt anything in years.

Look at your bride, you damn fool! Let her know you aren't just an ass with an agenda. That you're not merely King George's gutless son, forced into wedlock to get on with the business of begetting grandchildren! She deserves a real husband!

Pulling himself together, he turned. His smile was sudden and unanticipated, and he inhaled, oddly refreshed. Susan was walking toward him, lovely and lithesome. Her hair glowed like flame in the sunlight, the diamond-and-emerald tiara adding sparkle to a beauty that was so natural, so dazzling, he wanted to laugh out loud at his foolish doubts.

His bride was a vision in her slim, airy gown of ivory lace over silk. This winsome beauty moving slowly, gracefully in his direction was the same freckle-faced, live wire he'd proposed to. The same spitfire who'd doused him with orange juice and punched him, yet who'd quivered, naked under his devouring gaze the night he'd proposed.

It had been dark, but not *that* dark. No doubt his brief, shadowy glimpse played some role in his rushed proposal. But not the major role. Susan O'Conner had shown herself to be as resilient, bright and beautiful as any gemstone he could ever hope to hold. To allow her to slip through his fingers would be a crime.

Her wide blue eyes glimmered. The upturn of her lips seemed shy, even tentative. When his smile opened into a full-fledged grin, the hesitancy, if that's what he'd seen, vanished from her features, though a lovely blush emerged to heat his blood.

By the time her father stepped back to take a seat, and Susan stood by Jake's side, he took her hand without hesitation, lacing his fingers with hers. All of a sudden he felt quite possessive of the woman. *This is right,* he told himself, and squeezed her fingers, reassuringly.

As he spoke his vows, he experienced a stab of guilt. Adamantly he reminded himself that it would take time—this was a good thing, a new beginning.

So, before heaven and earth, Jake pledged his fidelity to Susan; though he knew—they both knew—Tatiana haunted his heart.

"You may kiss the bride."

Susan blinked and shot her gaze to Jake's face. She'd forgotten all about the traditional kiss. Jake faced her. Gently grasping her upper arms, he leaned down, his lips taking possession of hers.

That's when everything went black.

Susan didn't know how much time passed before she returned to her senses, but it must have been quite a while, for she and Jake were standing in a receiving line in the huge foyer. A strikingly handsome man had just taken her hand. She blinked, trying to focus. What had happened to her during that kiss?

Since nobody seemed to be staring or hovering around

with an IV needle, she decided she must not have actually passed out. But what—

"May I kiss the bride?" the handsome man asked, his dimpled smile reminiscent of Jake's. His hair was the same rich black as her husband's, though his eyes weren't green. His sparkling gaze was a rich, earthy brown. Impeccably dressed, he wore a conservative navy suit and power tie. He smelled clean, like soap and water. All in all, he was a handsome, charismatic package, and Susan instinctively knew he and Jake had to be family.

Her cheeks heated as he grinned at her. "I bet you're related to Jake," she said, her voice peculiarly breathy.

"Never saw him before in my life." He winked, leaning toward her and brushing a kiss on her cheek. When he straightened, he placed his other hand over the one he was already holding. "Actually I'm the handsome, brilliant, younger brother he's told you so much about."

She couldn't resist his breezy manner. It seemed the Merit family included more than one easygoing charmer. She'd never even heard that Jake had a brother. Obviously the Merit men kept their private lives very private. "Oh, of course," she teased back, "You're the *handsome* one." She peeked at Jake, surprised to note he was watching their exchange closely.

"Don't forget brilliant," the man reminded, slashing a crooked grin.

"And modest," Jake added, separating his brother's hands from his bride's. He smiled at her. "Susan, this is Marc. Youngest and least remarkable of the Merit sons. We threw him out years ago, but he keeps turning up like a bad penny."

Marc's laugh was rich, like his older brother's, and Susan grinned at the two as they bantered. "Now, now, old man," Marc said, "you know I come to all your weddings, even though I'm a very sought-after doctor."

Jake shook his head at his brother and bent closer to Susan's ear in a pretend whisper. "There isn't room on Merit Island for Marc and his ego. Just because he saves a life here and there…" Jake let the sentence trail off, then stepped forward, clasping his younger brother in a bear hug. "Thanks for coming, kid."

Susan could see Marc's face as they embraced. "I had a big morning saving lives." He winked at Susan. "So I figured I could go slumming this afternoon."

"I'm touched," Jake kidded. Releasing his brother, he stepped back.

Something in their conversation nagged at Susan's brain. "Youngest?"

When she realized Marc and Jake were no longer talking, but staring at her, she started. "Did—did I say something?"

Jake nodded. "You said 'youngest.'"

She smiled sheepishly. "Oh—I guess I was wondering why you'd called Mark the 'youngest' instead of 'younger' brother?"

"Oh—right," Jake said as he and Marc exchanged quick looks.

When neither spoke for a moment, she prodded, "Is there another brother I don't know about?"

"Actually there is," Marc said, once again glancing at Jake. "A middle brother, Zachary."

"Oh?" Susan asked, wondering at their hesitancy. "Where is he?"

Both brothers had lost their smiles. Jake inhaled, his lips thinned. "Zack left home a long time ago. He doesn't keep in touch."

Susan was startled. "You mean you don't know where he is or what he's doing?"

Jake smiled, though she detected a touch of melancholy in the expression. "Zack's the family rebel."

Realizing her questioning had brought down the mood, she tried for a joke. "Well, Jake, if Zack's a rebel, maybe you have a pirate in the family after all."

His grin was minimal. "I wouldn't be surprised." Turning back to his brother, Jake lay a hand on his shoulder. "Can you stay for a few days, kid?" His tone made it clear the touchy subject of Zachary Merit was closed.

Marc shook his head, his expression serious. "Wish I could. I miss the old place." He turned toward Susan and grinned full force. "Especially now that this lovely creature graces the island." He eyed his brother, skeptically. "I realize you're a wizened old codger, but I'd think even you would be too busy for the next few days to visit with me."

Glancing back at Susan, he bowed slightly, lifting her fingertips to his lips. "You have my deepest sympathy, sister dear," he teased. "I see a lifetime ahead of you filled with helping old Jake gum his oatmeal and reminding him what his name is."

A giggle bubbled in her throat. Marc Merit was an irresistible charmer. "You paint a grim picture. Perhaps I should rethink."

Marc shifted to eye Jake, his brows lifting playfully. "Just as I suspected. She's brighter than you deserve."

Jake's expression was one of mocking threat. "Why don't you go annoy father for a while?"

Marc lifted his chin and rubbed it as though struck. "You have a mean streak, old man. But I can take a hint." With one more, dashing wink at Susan, he moved along.

"I like Marc," she said as the last of the invited staff members made their congratulations.

Jake smiled. "And I like Yvette." His brows dipped, though he continued to smile. "Of course, you didn't bother to tell me you had a sister named Yvette—Susu."

She felt the impact of his mild reprimand. "You didn't bother to tell me you had a handsome, brilliant, doctor brother named Marc, either. Or a pirate brother named Zachary. Of course, I never *dated* either of your brothers…"

"If you're implying that I should have remembered you, be fair. You wore braces and glasses and they called you Susu."

He escorted her into the dining room and seated her to his right, at the head of the table. She glanced at him over her shoulder. "I outgrew the glasses and the braces. And business associates don't call me Susu."

He moved to his chair and took his seat. Leaning toward her, he covered her hand with his. "I take it then that calling you Susu will be one of my husbandly privileges?"

The underlying message of his query, and the huskiness of his voice, disconcerted her. Inhaling shakily, she stared into his eyes, not only riveting in their beauty but provocative in their message.

The memory of that look lingered in Susan's mind as Yvette helped her change out of her wedding dress. Ida Jean and Chester were with King George, who was playing Lord of the Manor, as he gave them a tour. George had been quite well-behaved this past week, and she sensed she knew why. He expected his first grandchild in nine months and fifteen minutes.

Susan experienced a warm glow come over her. For once she couldn't disagree with George. The idea appealed to her, too. Theoretically. But when she allowed herself to think about the reality of it, she flew into a panic. What if she disappointed Jake—physically? Or worse, what if he expected their marital bed to be nothing more than space reserved for sleeping and quick bouts of procreation, not for breathless adventures in passion? Since she held no emotional pull over his heart, what if he found his ease with other woman? What if—

"*Susu?*" Yvette gave her sister a shake. "Are you in there?"

Susan blinked, startled to realize she'd left the planet. "Uh, sorry. What were you saying?"

Yvette held up a short, green linen column dress with tiny embroidered roses all over it. "How about this for your going-away dress?"

Susan scanned it without interest. She and Jake were married! That was so earth-shattering in magnitude, she couldn't worry about a silly dress. "It's fine," she said absently.

Yvette laughed and tossed the dress on the bed along with several others. "You've said that about the last four."

Susan smiled wanly. "It doesn't matter what I wear. We're not going anyplace. Just—back up here."

"To Jake's bedroom." Yvette's smirk was knowing. She grabbed Susan's hands and pulled her to sit on the bed. "You know, Jake seemed genuinely surprised when I mentioned you'd been madly in love with him since you were fifteen."

Susan's stomach clenched. "What—did you say?" she whispered, praying she'd heard wrong.

"At least he just stared at me for a minute, so I assumed he was surprised." Yvette shrugged. "Didn't you tell him?"

Experiencing a clammy rush of mortification, Susan pulled her hands from her sister's. "Oh—my Lord!" Her face burned as she watched her life flash before her eyes. "What did he say?"

"Nothing much." Yvette looked confused. "What's wrong?"

"Tell me *exactly* what he said," Susan cried weakly.

Yvette scrunched up her face as though in thought. "Well—like I said, he seemed surprised at first, then he looked serious, then he smiled and said, 'Would you like some cake?'

"Would you like…" Susan's brain sizzled and snapped. She was sure the humiliating revelation had downed some very important wires. She could hardly think, and she was having trouble catching her breath. "That's all—just, 'Would you like some cake?'"

Yvette nodded. "Why? Didn't you want him to know about your crush?"

Mortified and furious, Susan cried, "You didn't say I had a crush on him when I was fifteen, you said I've loved him madly since I was fifteen. There's a difference!"

Yvette frowned. "So? He loves you and you love him. What's the matter—"

"He doesn't!" she blurted out, jumping to her feet. When she realized what she'd admitted out loud, her brave facade crumbled and she covered her face with her hands. "He doesn't love me!" she whispered brokenly, trying to wish the truth away. "He wants a family— children—and he's *comfortable* with me. That's why we're married. He doesn't love me, Vetie! He doesn't even know I love him."

After a long pause, Yvette whispered, "I don't believe this."

Susan swallowed hard. "Believe it."

"Oh dear." From the sound, Susan could tell her sister had stood. A moment later she felt Yvette's arms come around her, hugging her tight. "I'm so sorry, Susu. I hope—I wish…"

"Me, too," Susan moaned. Overcome by a miserable, rending despair, she clung to her sister and wept.

The wedding night loomed large in Susan's mind as she and Jake entered his bedroom. All the guests were gone, all the celebrating over. Next on the agenda: *The Honeymoon.*

"Well, this is it," Jake murmured.

Susan clasped her hands to hide their trembling. "This is it, all right," she mumbled. "The honeymoon."

He was silent for a moment, then remarked quietly, "That, too. But I meant, this is my room."

With a quick, embarrassed glance at his face, she shifted away. "Oh—of course." Self-conscious, she scanned his personal space. The bedroom floor was bleached white-oak planking, the walls tan. Comfortable and traditional furniture made the room both masculine and cozy.

Over the stone mantel of a large fireplace hung an oil painting of a strapping gentleman dressed in the silks and lace of a bygone era. Handsome, if a bit austere, he held the reins of a splendid sorrel stallion. Susan wondered if the horseman in the painting could be the ancestor who'd given England's King George the horse that netted the Merit family their island and subsequent fortune.

After hesitating as long as she could, Susan forced her gaze to the bed. It was large, like the man who slept there, with a headboard of old-fashioned wrought iron. Her doubts and fears surged to the surface and she pulled her gaze away, bouncing her focus to an unadorned pine dresser then down to muted, earth-tone throw rugs and on to the bank of arched windows that displayed a starry night. One window wasn't quite closed. The evening breeze wafted in, carrying light flowery scents mingled with the tang of the sea.

"It's a very nice room," she said, amazed at how composed she sounded, an unexpected miracle.

"Thanks." She felt his fingers slide down her arm to entwine with hers. "Susan?" He coaxed her to face him. "Don't be nervous."

She avoided his eyes. "I'm not."

"Come sit down." He paused, and though she wanted badly to judge his expression, she couldn't bring herself to look at him. "There's something I want to say," he finished.

She had a feeling she knew what was coming, but she decided to play dumb for as long as she could—maybe something other than the whole, mortifying truth would come to her that would explain away Yvette's "Susan's loved you madly since she was fifteen" remark.

When he tugged on her fingers, she cast him a surreptitious glance. His expression was serious, even vaguely annoyed. Oh, fine. The idea of being loved madly by Susan for thirteen years annoyed him! "Come. Sit." He drew her toward the bed. She obediently followed. They were married now—for better or worse. She was just sorry she had to start with worse.

He sat down, urging her to join him. Only when she'd taken a tentative seat as far away as his reach would allow did he let go of her fingers. Facing her, he pursed his lips as though measuring his words. In the waiting silence she inhaled feebly.

"Please relax," he said softly.

She peered at him. "Don't—don't I look relaxed?"

"Not very." He smiled, but it was only hinted at in his eyes, where she saw compassion rather than pleasure. She cringed at the sight. He was annoyed and he pitied her. Anguish seared her heart. "I don't want to make you nervous, Susan," he said. "So I think we should clear the air."

She nodded. "I think I know what you're going to say," she admitted.

"You do?" A brow rose. He seemed dubious.

"Yes." She dropped her gaze to her lap, watching her hands fidget. "I-I want to clear the air, too. To be per- fectly honest, I didn't—I don't—I ." This was so hard. Harder than any words she'd ever tried to put together into one coherent sentence.

"You didn't—don't—what?" he asked, his brows knitted with puzzlement.

"Okay, okay," she said through a forlorn sigh. "I did have a crush on you when I was fifteen, but I haven't been in love with you ever since." She blurted out the face-saving lie, hating the taste of it in her mouth. "Yvette's an incurable romantic, and she was wrong to say it. I just wanted to clear that up."

His expression grew pained for an instant, then eased. "I knew about the crush."

"You—knew?" She didn't know what she expected him to say, but it wasn't this. "Back then? You knew?"

He smiled and shrugged. "You were fifteen. Fifteen-year-old girls wear their hearts on their sleeves. Of course, I knew."

She was momentarily speechless with surprise. When she regained some of her mental function, she looked away, tears welling. "Oh—I'm so embarrassed."

"Why?" He touched her knee, drawing her gaze. She

stared down at his hand as he gently squeezed, telegraphing his reassurance. She fought the urge to cover his hand with her own. "I thought it was sweet," he said. When she looked up, his smile had disappeared, his expression solemn. "Why didn't you tell me you were my little Susu of so long ago?"

She was having trouble concentrating, with his hand on her leg. "I—I told you why. The fact that we'd met long ago had nothing to do with my job."

A muscle flexed in his cheek and he lifted his head in a half nod. "I guess I'll have to accept that, won't I?"

She sighed. "It's water under the bridge, anyway."

He frowned, then paused, looking troubled. "What Yvette said about you loving me madly." He quirked a rueful grin. "I was flattered, but..."

She bit her lip, positive she was reading his thoughts. *But I don't need that kind of pressure, Susan, especially right now. How can I possibly live up to your fantasy of me when I don't feel anything for you?* She cringed. How indeed?

"I told you, Yvette was mistaken!" she insisted, her expression as adamant as her tone. "Surely you know better, Jake." She swallowed, trying to get the shrillness out of her voice. "You know how our relationship came to be."

He removed his hand from her thigh and crossed his arms over his chest, his expression impossible to define. "Yes, I do." He shook his head. "Anyway, that brings me to my point."

Another point? "Oh?"

"I wanted to talk to you about—" He stopped, bared his teeth as though he was about to say something that was hard. Running a hand through his hair, he said, "I wanted to talk to you about sex, Susan."

The blood drained from her head and she felt dizzy. "Oh?" she squeaked, her heartbeat accelerating dangerously. "I—I thought you didn't discuss sex."

His serious expression altered slightly as her surprise remark made his lips quirk. "Not casually at the dinner table, no." His crooked grin seemed almost self-conscious. "But alone in my bedroom with my—wife. I think it's appropriate, don't you?"

She swept a loose strand of hair behind her ear. His logic was flawless. "So, what did you want to say about—it?" she asked, her voice quavery. She didn't know what she wanted to hear, she was scared and flustered and anxious and excited all at once. Which probably wasn't that much different from lots of brides.

His lips twisted wryly at her hesitance to say the word. He ran a hand across his jaw, the gesture contemplative. For a long confusing minute, he held her gaze. Suddenly he leaned forward, startling her by taking her face between his hands. His lips took possession of her mouth, causing her heart to leap perilously. His kiss was languid and tender and painfully brief, leaving her mouth burning for more.

He drew away slowly, his fingers lingering in her hair. She could only sit there and watch his withdrawal in stunned disbelief, her lips still parted and throbbing.

His hands slid along her face, down the column of her throat to rest lightly on her shoulders—a softly erotic act that set fire to her blood. "Susan," he murmured, "I think it's best that we take things slowly. By that I mean, I want you to be completely comfortable with me before we—" He gritted his teeth and inhaled sharply "—have sex."

Flummoxed by his declaration, she stared, experiencing a bombardment of muddled emotions. Her lips still tasted of him, and her skin, where his fingers had trailed, still tingled. Her body hummed with need. "Mmm," she said with a disjointed nod. Her response might not have made much sense, but it was the only answer she could conjure up for what she was feeling. Rejected? Aroused? Indignant?

A few heartbeats later, indignance won out. How dare he kiss her like he was going for the kissing championship of the world, then back away, basically telling her, *"By the way, I don't want you!"*

"I see," she murmured, choking back a lot of other words that tumbled and skidded around in her brain. Words like double-crosser and liar and piker! It was obvious Tatiana's memory still owned him—body and soul—and he couldn't bear the thought of being with his own wife!

"Wise decision," she murmured, maintaining her poise with difficulty. She tried to swallow, but her throat was as dry as dust. Feeling a threatening upsurge of tears, she vaulted from the bed. "So—I'll just be going to my room, then."

She'd made it two steps toward the exit before he caught her wrist. "No." He sounded grim. "I want you in my bed."

She peered at him, barely holding onto her composure. "Then where are you going to sleep," she asked, forcing herself to appear as though she hadn't just been trampled under the heel of his disinterest.

"Where am..." He let the sentence trail off, his expression darkening. What had he thought, that they wouldn't have sex but they'd sleep side by side? Why not? What was she to him? Certainly no one who might threaten to disturb his rest! "You're misunderstanding me."

She smiled benignly, her deep hurt billowing into an anger that gave her the strength to hide her pain. "I don't think so, Jake," she said quietly. "I understand perfectly. We're going to take things slowly. Wait until I'm—comfortable." Susan had never thought of a great sex life as something to be described as comfortable! Exciting, yes, exuberant, hopefully, even reckless. But comfortable? She never wanted it to be comfortable. Crossing her arms before her, she made her stance on the sleeping matter very clear. "I'm not sure when that will be, Jake. So where did you say you'd be sleeping?"

His nostrils flaring, he ground out, "I suppose I could—in my den."

That surprised her. "With all the bedrooms in this place, why sleep on a couch?"

"Because, I don't want the servants..." He pursed his lips, clearly trying to contain his temper.

She understood now. So he expected her to keep up their little pretense of a deliriously happy union. No one else must know the truth. No one else must realize Jake couldn't stand the idea of— "Afraid Daddy will disinherit you if he discovers you're not doing your *duty?*" she blurted out. Where had *that* come from? It was unfair, and unlike her. Of course, being rejected on one's wedding night might bring out the worst in almost anybody.

His eyes widened as though he'd been slapped, and she wished more than anything in the world she could call back her bitter jibe. Wanting to make amends, she shook her head. "Jake, I—"

"Good night, Susan," he cut in gruffly. With a brief, sidelong glance that chilled her to her core, he strode across the room and slammed into his private den.

CHAPTER TEN

JAKE bashed his shin on a low table in the dark den, the echo of the slamming door still ringing in his ears. "Blast it to hell!" he growled, kicking the stand out of his way. No matter what Susan might believe, Jake was spectacularly wealthy in his own right. Old George held precious little sway over him or any decisions he made. Ordinarily he could laugh off a comment like that, but just now he'd blown up. Why?

Sinking to the sofa, he massaged his leg, muttering, "What in blazes is wrong with me?" Slumping back, he shoved a hand through his hair, wanting to roar like a wounded lion. But the pain had nothing to do with his bruised shin.

He'd handled the situation with all the finesse of a rampaging gorilla. Rubbing his eyes with the heels of his hands, he wondered at his boorish behavior, stalking off and slamming out of the room. He didn't fly off the handle. He was usually logical and calm, hard to ruffle. So what made today so different?

He'd gotten married today, that's what. "Married…" he murmured, a sudden realization unnerving him. *The wedding kiss.* He might as well face it. That kiss was at least partly to blame for his behavior, which, to be blunt, seemed to have opened up a Pandora's box of major sexual frustrations.

During the ceremony, he hadn't planned to go beyond a whisperlike brush of her lips. Yet, before he knew what was happening, that brief, for-public-consumption, touch of her lips had become fiery and urgent. His mouth had met hers, then clung, moving in a lush exploration. Her kiss seared through him, filling him with unexpected passion, even wonder. And when he heard her small sound of surrender as her lips opened to him...

He winced, pushing back the recollection of his disorientation, then the peculiar sense of missing time. Since that moment when he'd held her in his arms, chancing upon such unforeseen physical excitement, he'd craved another taste. Perhaps his hunger showed, frightening her. Unfortunately his brain had still been consumed with the explosion of feeling her kiss had inspired.

It was entirely understandable that she'd assumed they would take more time to get to know each other before becoming physical. That had been his thinking, too— until the wedding kiss.

With a weary sigh, he slumped forward, resting his forearms on his knees. Without conscious thought, he glanced toward his bedroom and noticed the slash of light beneath the closed door. For a long time he stared at the golden strip of illumination. After a while it occurred to him that he hadn't heard a sound from in there. Not the creak of wood as she moved around, not the click of her heels nor the squeak of bedsprings. What was she doing, standing there glaring at the door?

In his mind's eye he could see her just as she was when he'd stalked out. She'd stood in the center of the room, watching him from beyond the gulf that had somehow formed between them. He recalled how her hair had caught the light, illuminating it with remarkable effect. She had thick, silky hair, a beautiful smile and a sexy blush. He'd never noticed until today how seductive such wholesome good looks could be.

He shook his head, angry with himself for bungling

everything so badly. "This isn't what I wanted, Susan," he muttered, his voice cracking with frustration. He'd wanted to make gentle love to her. He'd wanted to show her that if she truly had been in love with him, as Yvette suggested, then he would come to her as a real husband, do everything in his power to make her happy.

He'd tried to tell Susan that her sister's assertion had been flattering, but it had meant a great deal more to him than that, more than he'd ever thought it could. If his bride hadn't interrupted him, so adamant that none of it was true, then he would have told her so. Susan's insistence that Yvette had been wrong caught him right between the eyes.

He was suddenly at a loss, knocked off balance. So he'd made that lame speech about taking things slow, because that's what she needed to hear. Didn't she? "Yes!" he muttered. "Absolutely!" That was made obvious when his urgent hunger for her had made him go a little nuts, and he'd kissed her. Except for her shock, she hadn't reacted at all.

He ground his teeth. She'd never given him a single sign that she wanted him sexually. Well, except possibly that odd moment on the lawn after she'd tumbled on top of him. But even then he hadn't been sure which of them had initiated the movement that almost became a kiss. For all he knew, he could have unconsciously shifted closer. Damn! He'd thought about kissing her before then. He'd thought about it that first day she'd peeked into his office.

He peered at the bedroom door and noticed the light had been extinguished. Susan O'Conner Merit had gone to bed. His foul mood grew fouler and he ground out a curse. *His* wife was in *his* bed in *his* room in *his* home on *his* island! "Susu, dear heart," he vowed in a whispered growl, "Comfortable or uncomfortable, sex or no sex, if you think I intend to sleep on a godforsaken couch for the rest of my wedded life, you are sadly mistaken."

As the first week of their marriage dragged by, Susan became more and more depressed. Her panic over disappointing Jake had been far overshadowed by the sterile path their honeymoon had taken.

Her new husband invariably vanished into his dratted den at bedtime, asserting he had work to do. Then hours later when he assumed she was sleeping, he silently slipped into their bed. He fell asleep beside her, with his back to her, a painful message that her presence was less a comfort to him than an offense.

As the days passed, the sham was made doubly difficult by Jake's father. George's beaming expression and poorly veiled allusions about his anxiousness to hear the patter of little feet, were enough to make Susan want to tear her hair and scream.

Publicly Jake behaved like a devoted husband—smiling, taking her arm or holding her hand. In private, his manner was quiet and brooding. It was excruciatingly obvious that Tatiana's memory still had too great a hold. What other reason could there be for him to relinquish the physical side of marriage? Despondent, Susan felt sure he planned to stall until he was so in need of sexual release, even *she* looked good.

After two weeks, Susan thoroughly dreaded their bedtime ritual—of mute, embarrassing maneuvers to keep out of each others' way. Of mumbled exchanges and short bursts of uneasy eye contact, as they came and went between bedroom and bath. Of Jake's inevitable departure to his den. Of the long, lonely hours staring into darkness, wishing…wishing…yet knowing she had no right to wish. Hadn't she entered into this perverse arrangement with her eyes wide-open?

That evening, as usual, Susan had the bathroom to herself to bathe and get ready for bed, since Jake always showered and changed before dinner. Just as she was about to enter the bath, Jake came in. Their glances clashed for an overlong moment before he nodded solemnly and walked to the open window to stare out to sea. Her heart constricting, she hurried into the bathroom before Jake could witness her tears.

After a long, calming soak in the tub, Susan dried off and wrapped the towel about her. Listlessly she plucked her toothbrush from its holder on the marble countertop and pulled out the drawer beside her sink. No toothpaste. "Oh, right," she mumbled, remembering she'd used the last of the tube this morning. Checking around, she tried to recall where extra toiletries were stored. Her gaze caught on a shelf over his sink.

She opened the cabinet and spotted several boxes of toothpaste, stuck far back on the middle shelf. Rising up on tiptoe, she grasped one. It wasn't until too late that she noticed she had dislodged a glass bottle. When realization hit, so did the bottle—a glancing blow to her collarbone. The container slammed into the edge of the sink, shattering with a deafening crash. Glass shards and the bottle's innards flew everywhere.

Susan cried out in pain and fright, instinctively massaging the place the bottle struck her. A millisecond later she felt cool lotion spatter her chest and legs. The scent of almond filled the air.

Too stunned to make sense out of what had happened, she reflexively glanced down at herself. A throbbing red spot marred her collarbone. Confused, she touched a dot of the ointment that spattered her chest. Hand lotion?

The bathroom door burst wide. "What happened? Are you okay?"

Startled by Jake's abrupt appearance, she lurched, tipping over. The instant before she moved her foot to regain her balance, her brain screamed, *Don't! You'll cut yourself to ribbons,* which was easier said than done. The top half of her body was already toppling.

Options being in pitifully short supply, she grabbed for the closest solid object, which happened to be Jake. "Don't let me fall!" she cried, seizing his shoulders in a death grip.

He lifted her off the glass-littered tiles, and everything went oorily still. Even her heart. Their eyes met, his expression perplexed. For a pulse beat he broke eye contact to examine her. When he looked up, his eyes seemed dilated and a muscle jumped in his cheek. "What happened?"

"I—I was getting toothpaste. Something fell off the shelf." She indicated the offending cupboard, but his glance didn't move. "I think—it was hand lotion," she went on. "I'm sorry. There's glass everywhere."

She released him with one arm, planning to smooth the cream into her skin. Glancing down, she noticed her towel had slipped, bearing her breasts. *"Oh!"* She yanked, but the towel didn't budge. The dratted thing had become twisted in her leap for life. Horrified, she snatched her other arm from around his neck to cover herself. "Oh—no..." Her gaze shot to his. How humiliating! How mortifying! *"Please, Jake, put me down!"*

His eyes narrowed as though he was in pain. Beads of perspiration glistened on his forehead. "Damn it, Susan, the floor's covered with glass," he muttered. Without further debate, he swept her into their room and carried her to the bed.

As soon as he lay her on the spread, she started to scramble away. "Thanks, I'm—"

"I'd better check you for cuts," he broke in, placing a restraining hand on her shoulder. "Lie still." His glower was so ominous, she did as he said. Snagging the towel, she pulled it up to cover her breasts and nervously watched as he sat on the edge of the bed and began to examine her legs. His thumb skimmed over her skin as he explored, sending a thrill through her. She bit her lower lip, turning her face away. "What was in the bottle?" she asked, trying to get her mind on something beside his touch.

"Aftershave balm." His hand gently closed over her ankle, and she became aware that he was rubbing the stuff into her skin. "It won't hurt you."

Slowly, painstakingly, he massaged up along her leg to where her towel had protected her. She shifted to peer at him, struck by the beauty of his profile. So serious in his concentration. She found herself reclining back, admiring the way his lips turned down sensually at each corner. Without a word or a look, he shifted his ministrations to her other leg, gently working the cool balm into her skin.

She swallowed. His touch engendered a warm tingle deep inside her that was impossible to ignore. After another moment, he turned. Their eyes met, and she knew he sensed her reserve just as she sensed his. She studied him silently for what seemed like an eternity as glittering, green eyes studied her back.

Suddenly the tattered remnants of her self-restraint vanished and she was neither embarrassed nor fearful. She only knew she loved Jake Merit. She loved the curve of his mouth, the tenderness in his eyes and the supple strength of his hands. She loved him—good, bad or indifferent.

She loved him. There was nothing more to be said.

His expression changed somehow, disclosing an emotion stronger than mere masculine interest. Without a word, he leaned toward her. Placing one palm on her shoulder, he began to smooth the spattered lotion into her flesh. His glance shifted to her other shoulder, and his frown deepened. "Is that a bruise?"

Her throat closed with yearning and she could do no more than nod.

Their glances touched for only an instant, but long enough for her to see a flame of something raw and real leap to life in his eyes. He leaned forward, and to Susan's amazement, tenderly kissed her reddened flesh. The staggering sweetness of the act sent fire through every nerve in her body, and she quivered with it.

Sweet, slow kisses moved along her collarbone to the moist hollow of her throat, triggering wild, primitive longings inside her.

"Jake?" she whispered, not daring to hope.

"Shh," he cautioned softly as he nipped along her throat to her jaw.

When at last he brushed her lips with his, the contact held a tender yet galvanizing message, propelling another hot wave of desire through her.

His kisses were surprisingly sensitive, light and questing, driving her mad. The virile nearness of his body made her flesh sizzle, and her need for him became primal, overwhelming, the stuff of legends and love songs. Parting her lips, she challenged him to possess her mouth.

Exhaling a ragged groan, he accepted.

Arousing and tantalizing, his fingers trailed down her throat and over the rise of her breast. The brush of his hand along the edge of fabric was poignant in its restraint. She reacted bizarrely, her consciousness ebbing as her desire raged hotter.

Jake made a guttural sound, half-growl, half-moan. Then suddenly, with a bold flick of his wrist, he swept her towel away.

The wonder of Jake's lovemaking staggered Susan to such a degree she found herself crying. She'd never known this intense fulfillment, this astounding completeness, never realized such an exalted state of being existed.

Even as Jake lay above her, their bodies and souls conjoined, ragged sobs of joy escaped her lips. All her hopes and dreams, as wild and impossible as they seemed, had finally, gloriously, come to be.

Jake had relaxed, blanketing her, his potent strength a divine burden. With her sobs, he lifted his head, his expression somewhere between contentment and apprehension. "Susan?" Misgiving tinged his whisper.

Sated from lovemaking, her arms were too heavy to lift, though she badly wanted to run her fingers through his mussed hair. Smooth the slight wrinkle from his brow. Her lips tremulous, she whispered, "Jake—" A new sob broke off her assurance, and tears streamed from her eyes, dampening the rumpled sheets.

His eyebrows dipped, and he squeezed his eyes shut. Releasing a heavy sigh, he rolled away to sit slumped on the side of the bed, his back to her.

"Jake?" She stretched out an arm, beseeching, but couldn't quite reach him. *He regretted making love to her!* She felt instantly cold, empty, abandoned. "We're married..." she assured in a quivery whisper, "...you had every right—"

"Hell!" he interrupted, "I know my husbandly rights." He pushed up from the bed and grabbed her towel, wrapping it about his waist. His need to hide himself hurt as much as the harshness in his tone, the regret in his voice. "I also know all about family duty!" Jerking a hand through his hair, he turned to confront her. "I—didn't want..." His jaw worked; his nostrils flared. Breaking eye contact, he shook his head. "I didn't mean—"

"Don't," she cried. *"Please!"* Tugging at the sheet, she reluctantly covered herself. The last thing she wanted to hear was an apology from her own husband for making love to her. What a pitiful, lovesick fool she was. He'd exercised his rights as her husband, done his duty to his family, and now he felt derelict to his memory of...

Just thinking the word Tatiana shattered her. A dull ache began to form in her core, where only moments ago she had glowed with contentment and oneness with the man she loved.

In self-defense, she allowed him to see her simmering hurt. "There's no need to feel guilty, Jake," she said flatly. "Sex was part of the deal. From what I understand, it's the usual method men and women use to produce offspring." Her lips trembled, and she pressed her hands over her face. Stifling a sob, she grew furious with herself for giving in to defeat and forced a choked laugh. "You actually—*performed* quite well. Considering the calculated nature of our—" Clearing the tremor from her voice she hurried on, "—our marriage. If there had been any real caring between us, the experience might have been—" Overcome with a sadness so profound, the lie stuck in her throat and she turned away.

"Adequate?" he finished, his tone low and hoarse.

Unable to trust her voice, she executed a hideous fraud, and nodded.

CHAPTER ELEVEN

JAKE felt like a heel. He'd expected to have the self-control to wait for Susan to show *some* sign of willingness, before…

He ground out a low oath. How could he have lost control? Though he was shocked with himself, he experienced a certain ironic pleasure, too. The realization unsettled him. How big a bastard did that make him? How could he be pleased, considering what a selfish pig he'd been? A small voice in the back of his mind jeered, *You're pleased because the sensual Susan excites you far more than you could have imagined.*

That was the good news. The bad news was that Susan now watched him warily whenever he entered a room. Though they continued to impersonate happy newlyweds in public, she colored fiercely when he took her hand. The sight never failed to rekindle, in Jake, heated memories of the lovemaking they'd shared. He was a man in pain—a pain he'd brought on himself.

Susan thanked providence that she still had her work, though now her position had become exclusive to Merit Emeralds, her job location, the island. As things now stood, she and Jake spent their days together on the job, and their nights together, too. Though work occupied her mind during the day, it didn't eradicate the torment of being near Jake almost every waking moment. Neither did it give her any respite from inhaling his scent, of feeling the warmth of his hand or hearing his rich, deep laughter while joking with employees. She was a woman in pain—a pain she'd brought on herself.

Though in public Jake played the loving husband, he kept his distance once they were alone in their room. As the days passed, Susan's frustration built to explosive proportions. Obviously she hadn't been what he'd wanted or needed in a...she frowned, unwilling to think about how utterly she'd failed him.

A suffocating sensation tightened her throat. *Failure!* She wasn't a failure! Susan O'Conner had never been a failure at anything she'd really wanted to do. How dare she accept Jake's name, then immediately attach that horrible label to it. "Susan O'Conner Merit," she muttered, "you will not be a failure in your marriage!"

She was Jake's wife. Being a wife held certain responsibilities, especially in their situation. Jake had married her to move on with his life. The fact that she had found a framed photograph of Tatiana stuck in the back of a drawer in his bedside table, didn't enter into it. He'd never lied to her about his feelings.

She knew how he felt, but she also knew how *she* felt. She loved Jake. They both wanted children. She wanted his children. She wanted to believe that once she was pregnant, and they were bonded together by an impending birth, they would become closer. She would truly be his partner, then, and he would begin to think of her as more than a substitute wife and surrogate mother. She had to cling to that belief or go mad!

She'd felt a little strange lately. Did she dare hope she might be pregnant, already? Could a woman tell after only one week?

Mustering her courage, she turned the knob of their bedroom door and walked inside. She knew Jake's schedule by now and wasn't surprised to see him turn abruptly at the sound. When he saw her, he hurriedly finished slipping on a casual polo. "Susan?" he asked, looking concerned. "Is something wrong?"

She usually spent this time of day meandering through one of the extensive gardens, or strolling by the sea, so she wasn't surprised by his confusion. She shook her head. "Nothing's wrong…" Her voice caught. That was a lie. Something was very wrong. Heat rushed up her cheeks and she swallowed to ease the dryness in her throat. "Jake?"

As he finished tucking his shirt into his khakis, he turned to face her directly. "Yes?"

Red-golden rays from the evening sun gave him a crown of light. Even with the brightness behind him, his eyes glimmered. How could he seem more striking every time she saw him?

During the drawn-out silence, he tilted his head in a coaxing gesture. "Tell me." His jaw flexed and he folded his arms before his chest, as though preparing for a confrontation.

No! No! she cried inwardly. *I don't want to fight with you, Jake. I want to love you! I want you to love me!* Forcing herself to calm down, she faced him unflinchingly. "Jake, I'm your wife," she said with quiet resolve. "I agreed to our bargain."

His only reaction was the slight lift of an eyebrow.

"I just want…" In the face of his skepticism, she could feel her resolve slipping, but she fought to hold on. Why was it that Jake, of all people in the world, could make her mind turn to mush? "I want…" Determined though she was, she could no longer meet his gaze. Still, she refused to abandon her effort. She'd done enough failing lately to last her a lifetime. She shuddered and clenched her hands together. "I just want—"

"That's the third time you've said that," he cut it, brusquely. "What is this thing you want?"

Her glance shot to his face, her pulse rate doubling. Was he angry? Why? She opened her mouth, but no sound came and her lip began to tremble. Licking them, she sucked in a breath. "I'm *saying,* I intend to be your wife—in every sense of the word—whenever you feel—" she swallowed. "—the need."

She tried to hold eye contact, show him how desperately she meant what she said. But she panicked, afraid if he saw the raw longing in her eyes it would only make him more aggravated than he already was. He had enough pressures, from his father and his dedication to Tatiana's memory, without thrusting the weight of her unrequited love on his shoulders.

She dropped her gaze to her clasped hands. The tension that reverberated around the room seeped into Susan's body, making her feel insubstantial, as though her bones were made of cotton. After an interminable amount of time, she heard the tap of his shoes as he approached.

Large, warm hands gently took hold of her upper arms; a light kiss grazed her forehead. "I have a few calls to make, Susan," he murmured, releasing her. "I'll see you at dinner."

She couldn't move. Even after the door clicked shut at his back, she merely stood there, just as she'd been when he brushed her off with that chaste kiss. After a time, her legs gave way and she sank to the floor.

A reprieve. Ridiculously relieved, Jake came close to hugging the butler. Susan hadn't asked for an annulment, after all. So much for male intuition. He'd been positive that was the point she was nervously stammering toward.

Her little speech left a lot to be desired as far as his

ego was concerned. But she was sticking by their agreement, and she was sticking by him. Because of her shy assurance, he felt more optimistic. He could give her a little more time—time to rebuild what he'd damaged with his rashness. "What's wrong with you, man?" he grumbled curtly to himself once he was alone in his office. "You're not rash. As a matter of fact, you're damned near indifferent about most things. Ever since—" He cut himself off, but his thoughts trailed on. *Ever since Tatiana died.*

For twelve years, he'd grieved for her, mooned over her. He'd poured all his energies into his work so he could keep his focus narrow. Mining emeralds and polishing Tatiana's memory had been his whole life. He'd killed off every latent thought, every rudimentary human connection, if it didn't lead him straight back to his work or his memories.

Then Susan O'Conner appeared in his self-made island fortress. She had tossed a wrench in the well-oiled machinery of his sterile reality, making him see what a barren wasteland his life had become.

He would always be grateful to her for the insight, no matter how painful it had been to accept. That was the major reason he'd asked her to marry him. Curiously, somewhere along the way, gratitude had taken a back seat to more powerful emotions. He wanted her, now, more than he could imagine he would want any woman besides Tatiana. And if pressed, he wasn't sure even Tatiana would measure up, after Susan's brave speech.

His gut twisted with desire and self-disgust. She was willing to have sex with him because it was her duty. She'd been so determined, yet she hadn't been able to mask her distress. Watching her make such a valiant gesture filled him with a mix of crazy hope and dismay.

He'd been hard-pressed not to take her right then and there. But blast it, he wasn't going to jump her again, like a rutting bull. Next time they would come together mutually. Next time, he vowed, he would see desire in her eyes.

An idea struck, and he stilled in thought. For weeks he'd put off a business trip to Antwerp. Perhaps this would be a good time to go—give her a few days of peace, without him always there, making her nervous. If absence truly made the heart grow fonder, then he had great hopes for his homecoming.

Susan was furious with herself. She'd allowed her desperate love for Jake to make her a mealymouthed weenie, again! She was his wife, for heaven's sake! She had every right to bring about her own happiness, her own satisfaction.

Jake hadn't changed his sleeping pattern, spending much of last night in his den. Susan had lain awake plotting a seduction of her own. Today, drilling came to an end early for some minor maintenance work on the rig. Susan had already left instructions in the kitchen to prepare a picnic dinner for her and Jake. The late September weather was exceptionally mild, and the trees were a riot of fall colors.

She had the spot picked out, deep in the woods, with a clearing that overlooked the ocean. Yet, it was safely out of the watchful eye of security cameras. Jittery and excited, she bathed early, waiting for Jake to finish some calls in his office. The moon would be nearly full, and there wasn't a cloud in the sky.

"Tonight, Susan!" she whispered to herself as she slipped on a silk cardigan as a blouse. Buttoning only the first three buttons, she left a bit of skin peeping out above her short, wrap skirt. She smiled to herself. Wouldn't Jake be surprised when he discovered she didn't have on a scrap of underwear! "Oh, Susan," she whispered through a giggle. "You're a sly vixen."

"Did you say something?"

She whirled to see Jake standing in the doorway, his expression vaguely concerned.

"I—I—" *Do it now!* she told herself. *Tell him about the picnic! He's through with work for the day.* "I thought we might have a picnic."

He cocked his head, his brow wrinkling. "A picnic?"

She inhaled, sucking in a draught of courage. "Yes, I—"

"That would be great," he said, heading for his closet. "One of these days." He disappeared inside. "I have to leave for Antwerp in a few minutes."

She blinked, baffled. What had he said?

"I'll be gone for about a week." When he reappeared, he held a leather suitcase. His gaze narrowed, he observed her for a second before tossing the bag on the bed. "I'm sorry about this, but if I don't go now, it'll be a month before my gem broker and I can get together again. It can't wait that long." He flipped the latches and opened the bag before glancing her way. His smile was painfully diplomatic. His eyes slightly narrowed, so she couldn't read them. "Would you grab my shaving kit out of the bathroom?"

She felt a dullness settle in her chest, of disappointment or disbelief, or both. He was leaving, just like that? Numb, she nodded to his request, and retrieved his shaving gear. When he noticed she'd returned, he took it from her with a brief smile. "Thanks."

She nodded again, a scream of frustration welling in her throat. Her carefully planned seduction was to have

been tonight! "This—trip," she said, working to keep
her voice even. "It came up suddenly?" She didn't want
to believe he'd been driven to trumping up fake business
jaunts to get away from her.

"No, not really." He walked to his dresser. Scooping
up an armload of underwear and socks, he returned and
dropped them into the suitcase. "I've needed to go, but
I haven't had time." Snapping the lid closed, he fastened
the latches and straightened. He peered at her for a heartbeat, seeming to consider saying more. A look came over
his face that Susan could only describe as grim determination.

With a quick, almost nonexistent shake of his head, he
grabbed his bag. In two strides he stood before her,
brushing a kiss on her lips. "The hotel's name and num-
ber are on my desk. Call if you need anything." His eyes
met hers, a breathtaking sight, brilliant, beautiful and
darkly fringed. "I'll see you in a week," he murmured,
before making a swift exit.

Confused, frustrated and hurt beyond words, Susan
wandered restlessly around the room. If this so-called
business trip hadn't been sudden, then why hadn't he
mentioned it? She found herself at the window, and
leaned forward to rest her forehead against the cool glass.

There he was, striding along the dock toward one of
his cruisers. She clutched the sill. "Why are you leaving
me, Jake?" she whimpered, unable to staunch her tears.
"I want to be your wife. In—in every sense—" A sharp
pain squeezed her belly and she groaned. Wincing, she
bit her lip and took a quick couple of breaths. She'd felt
worse and worse every day for the past week. Was she
getting an ulcer?

Another stitch made her double over. "Oh, *Jake*," she
cried weakly. "Please—please, don't be sorry you mar-

ried...'' This time the stab of discomfort made her cry out, and she stumbled to the bed.

What was happening? Was her pain purely emotional, or was something very, very wrong?

CHAPTER TWELVE

JAKE had only been gone for five days, but to Susan it was a lifetime. When he'd left, her only thought was finding a way to get him to come to her as a husband, to make love to her, so their mutual goal to have children, become a real family, could come true.

Today, all that was crushed. Today, she had nothing to offer Jake that he wanted from her. Today, she'd received the results of the tests Dr. Fleet insisted she have done. When he'd given her the news, he'd been very kind, looking as sad as if she had been his own daughter.

"Rapid-onset Endometriosis" was a big label for a condition that essentially meant Susan couldn't have children. She'd received the diagnosis four hours ago, but it had taken that long for the full impact to penetrate.

The shock and grief left her desolate. Jake had married her for the *children* she would bear him. But, now...

The pain in her heart gnawed at her as she struggled against a reality too cruel to allow fully into her consciousness. The bitterness of it almost suffocated her and she had to gasp for air.

The depth of her love for Jake, by itself, had never been enough—just a silly pipe dream she'd allowed herself to dream for a time. Without the promise of babies, their marriage deal was dead. Even an idiot could see he'd married her with defined expectations, expectations she could no longer fulfill. She might as well be adult about it, stop wailing and weeping, and do what had to be done.

She wasn't sure when Jake would get back from Antwerp. She hadn't called him, though he'd called her. They'd spoken on the phone the first couple of nights after he left. Their conversations had held sporadic silences and uncomfortable gaps. After that, she'd made sure she was outside when he'd called.

She couldn't stand to tell him she'd been to a hospital for tests. She couldn't allow herself to think about the consequences of such a revelation, since talking about trivialities had been awkward enough. So, she'd walked aimlessly through the woods, praying she had an ulcer or some weird kind of stomach flu, and when Jake returned their picnic could go on as planned.

But now, with the awful truth staring her in the face, she knew there would be no happy reunion, no seduction in the woods. As she hurriedly packed a suitcase, she tried to rationalize her cowardly escape. It would be easier on him this way, she told herself, not to have to advise her that since she wasn't able to live up to their bargain the marriage was null and void.

She couldn't stand hearing the words, seeing his detached expression, his shuttered eyes. Being a genuinely kind man, it would be difficult for him. Perhaps not the heartbreaking desolation she felt, but difficult. She could only take so much, and she couldn't take being labeled deficient and set aside by the man she'd loved half her life.

Her hands trembling, she snapped her suitcase closed, deciding to send for the rest of her things. A sparkle caught her attention and she grew still, staring at the wedding band on her left hand. Her heart constricted, though not because the ring was a costly treasure she would regret leaving behind. It was admittedly lovely, with channel-set diamonds running the entire circumference of the band, and a square-cut, three-carat diamond as its crowning glory.

No. Her pain was because of what the ring symbolized, all the hopes and dreams it carried with it that now would never come true.

Her throat aching with the need to cry, she tugged the band off her finger and lay it on the linen spread. With difficulty she dragged her gaze away. Tugging the battered old suitcase off the bed, she headed for the door. When it suddenly opened, she stumbled with surprise. "Jake?" His name came out in a fragile, dismayed thread. Why did Fate demand that she face one, final catastrophe?

He noticed her suitcase and his smile of greeting dimmed. "What's going on?"

Seeing him standing there was pure agony. Clad in black, he looked so solid, the powerful set of his shoulders filling the doorway. She stared, mute and miserable.

He lifted a brow, looking uncertain. "Susan?" He said her name quietly, as though concerned that any noise might spook her.

When she didn't say anything, he came close, and looked down at her, his eyes questioning. "You look so—is someone in your family ill?"

She shook her head, experiencing a stab at the irony of his question. "No—Jake..." The scent of his aftershave wreaked havoc on her convictions, but she battled down her desire. "I'm leaving you." She hurried on, afraid if she didn't say it all, and say it quickly, she would melt into a puddle at his feet and plead for his love. "Our

marriage was a mistake," she said, brokenly. "I'm divorcing you. Don't fret, I don't want anything. Just — *out.*"

"Susan?"

As she turned toward the door, he took hold of her arm, but she yanked away. "Don't!" She eyed him with as much feigned hostility as she could muster. "And don't follow me. My mind is made up."

His brows knit, his expression bewildered.

When the door closed between them, he didn't follow. As she boarded the Merit cruiser, he was nowhere to be seen.

Good, she told herself. *This is best. A nice, clean, uncomplicated break.*

She made herself turn away from Merit Island to stare at the heaving ocean. "A nice, clean, uncomplicated break," she whispered, swiping away a tear.

Jake felt betrayed, as though his wife had left him. He laughed caustically. "She did, you fool."

Damnation! He wasn't a man to go chasing after a woman. She'd made her decision for whatever reason. It was none of his concern. Just because she could knock a man to his knees with a karate punch didn't mean she was strong enough to stay in a marriage that didn't suit her.

He ran a hand across his eyes, for the thousandth time trying to banish memories of her soft, sweet lovemaking. "Maybe it would have been kinder if she'd left me standing at the altar like the others," he muttered.

Two weeks passed. Two tedious, hard weeks. He tried to move on with his life, but everything he did, everywhere he went on the island, held memories of Susan.

Especially that outcropping of rock, where he'd pulled her from the ocean.

And his blasted bed!

"Hell!" he ground out, as he approached the bottom of the staircase. Another workday endured, it was finally time for dinner. But Jake wasn't hungry. He was angry. More like furious. Why couldn't he put Susan from his thoughts?

The irony of his misbegotten love life gnawed at him. For so many years he'd mourned Tatiana. Without his realizing it, the bereavement had become a habit. His grief for his lost Tati had become nothing more than a shell, a place for him to retreat, so he wouldn't have to deal with the real world and real relationships. He'd been blind to that fact until Susan came into his life and knocked the dust off a fixation that should have been purged long ago. But now that he finally understood all that, he'd lost Susan.

Out of the corner of his eye he noticed one of the servants do an about-face and quickly skitter the other way. He scowled, muttering, "What in Hades is wrong with everybody lately? They run away as though I had the plague!"

"Jake, my boy, you'd better watch that temper or you'll get an ulcer."

Jake hadn't noticed Dr. Fleet idling beside the living-room entry. He stopped and glared at the wizened old man. "And to what do we owe this visit? I don't remember calling a doctor?"

The older man squinted at Jake, his expression announcing he was no great fan of sarcasm. "I was invited to dinner. But if you're going to snap at me, I'll just go home and avoid you like everybody else."

Jake's scowl deepened. "Nobody's avoiding me!" He wasn't sure he believed that, but it wasn't Dr. Fleet's business if they were.

"Oh?" Dr. Fleet asked, his shaggy brows quirking upward. "So, what was that kitchen lad doing just then when he came to a skidding halt and hightailed it back in the opposite direction?"

"How in blazes would I know? He probably forgot something."

The doctor's eyebrows didn't move. They stayed raised in incredulity for a long, telling moment, before they crinkled in a frown. "It's your life, son. Handle it as you please." He shook his head. "Give George my apologies, but I don't think I'll stay for dinner, after all. Emma already declined. She doesn't like seeing you this way."

"What way?" Jake bellowed, annoyed at being treated like a rebellious child. "Doc, you may have been on this island since before I was born, but that doesn't give you any right to—"

"*That* way!" Elmer cut in. "Lately you've done nothing but roar like a testy lion. You've put your father's crankiness to shame with your thundering." He looked as though he might say something more, but instead he frowned and shook his head. "Oh, never mind. Talking to you is like talking to a pile of bricks." He turned away, muttering something Jake couldn't quite catch.

"What?" he barked.

The slump-shouldered old physician turned on Jake, his features florid. "I said, I knew you could be a harsh, but to send your wife away because she can't have children. That's *despicable!*"

The doctor's accusation slammed Jake in the gut like

a wrecking ball. "What—did you say?" His tone was edged with disbelief and denial. "What in blazes do you mean?"

"You know darn well what I mean!" he retorted, angrily.

Jake stared, his gut constricting. "I didn't want her to leave, blast it! What are you babbling about?"

"But, I thought…" Dr. Fleet looked closely at the younger man, his expression troubled. "Surely she told you, Jake. I figured that was why…" The doctor's features distorted with self-reproach. He shook his head, plainly remorseful for betraying a patient's confidence. "*Damnation!*" he muttered. "Since your bride evidently didn't want you to know, you'll have to ask her."

In no mood for games, Jake clamped his hands on Dr. Fleet's shoulders, 'Guess again, Doc!" he growled.

CHAPTER THIRTEEN

RUNNING on pure adrenaline, Jake made Portland in record time. He burst into Susan's office, but she wasn't there. Her boss, Ed Sharp, informed Jake that Susan had accepted a job in California, and was leaving on a flight that evening.

Jake arrived at the airport gate to find all but a few straggling standby passengers had already boarded the plane. He stalked to the attendant monitoring the entrance to the gangway. "I have to get on that flight," he said.

The woman looked startled by his vehemence. "Certainly, sir." She held out a hand. "I'll just need to see your boarding pass."

"I don't have one. I'm not going anywhere." He pushed a hand through his hair. "I have to get somebody off that plane."

The attendant gave him a dubious look. "I'm sorry, sir. No one is allowed on the plane unless they have a boarding pass."

He clamped his jaws shut to keep from saying something that would get him hauled away by airport security. He tried to gather his calm. "Look, it'll just take one minute."

"I'm sorry, sir." She glanced at a man who had walked up to them. "Yes?"

"I was standby, but they called my name."

The attendant held out her hand. "Your boarding pass?"

Jake had no intention of being kept off that plane. There had to be a way. An idea came to him and he yanked off his emerald ring and thrust it toward the smaller man who held the coveted boarding pass. "Look, buddy, this ring is worth sixty thousand dollars. It's yours—for that pass."

The stand-by passenger's gaze darted from Jake's face to the ring, then back to his face. Seconds ticked ponderously by, and Jake was quickly running out of patience. "For what this ring is worth, you can charter your own damn plane."

"Well..." The man hesitated.

"It's a Merit emerald," he added, annoyed by the man's indecision. "I'm Jake Merit."

He heard a gasp and his glance slid to the attendant. "You *are!*" Her mouth sagged open and she turned to the standby passenger. "He *is!*" she whispered in awe. "I recognize his face from news stories."

Both attendant and passenger turned wide-eyed attention to the ring in Jake's hand.

"Sure...sure..." the smaller man said, "I guess I could take—"

"Fine." Jake tugged the pass from the man's fingers and slapped the ring in his palm. "Thanks."

Shifting toward the gawking attendant, he stuck the boarding pass into her hand and ran down the access ramp to the plane.

Susan fastened her seatbelt without much interest. Her mind was too numb. She was leaving for a place she'd never been, to be with people she'd never met, to take a job she didn't want, in order to escape a man she loved more than life itself. She sighed heavily, drawing the curious gaze of her closest seatmate, a rotund man in his forties. She blessed him when he turned back to his *Wall Street Journal* without speaking.

Leaning back, she closed her eyes, praying that she would quickly get wrapped up in the dynamics of taking a new job and living in a new place. Surely all that newness would help ease her despair and loneliness. Eventually.

She didn't hope for a quick fix, just a gradual lessening of the pain.

"Mrs. Merit?"

Susan jumped, her eyes going wide. That was Jake's voice! Her aisle seat was located halfway back from the entry to Coach Class. Peering toward the front, she was dumbfounded to see him blocking the entry, legs braced wide, hands gripping either side of the partition, as though he had no intention of allowing anyone to pass without his express permission. His features were intent, determined. His jaw was set, his emerald gaze snapping with purpose. Lord, he was glorious.

"I'm looking for my wife—Susan Merit," he said, searching faces in her compartment.

When their eyes met, she physically felt the impact. When Jake looked at you, you *knew* it! Something raw and beautiful passed across his features. Releasing the partitions, he rushed to her. "What do you think you're doing, Susan?"

Too stunned to respond, she could only stare.

In another shocking turn, Jake knelt beside her, taking

her hand. His grasp felt so warm, so welcome. She hadn't realized how cold she'd felt—for days and days. "Susan," he whispered huskily. "I thought we were partners."

Regaining some of her wits, she forced herself to recall why she'd left him. Struggling to remain unaffected, she pulled her gaze from his. "It—it was a bad idea. It wouldn't work."

"It was working for me," he said softly.

"Really?" Unable to help herself she faced him. "A husband shouldn't have to force himself to...to..." She couldn't go on. Everybody was staring.

"I forced myself *not* to, darling," he murmured, his eyes glimmering with emotion. "I didn't want you to feel—pressured. I was ashamed of myself that one time—when you—cried."

His quiet admission floored her, but she battled back any softening. She couldn't give him children, and that had been his whole reason for marrying her. There was nothing to discuss. "You don't understand." In the hushed stillness of the cabin, her words seemed overloud.

He took her face in his hands. "I understand that I love you, Susan," he whispered, apparently not caring that they were the center of attention. Even the flight attendants stood frozen and gaping. "I love you, Susan," he repeated, his voice low and urgent. "That's all I need to understand."

Tears of agony filled her eyes. Those were the words she'd wanted to hear so badly for so long. Why did they have to come when it was too late? Jerking from his grasp, she cried, "Please! Just go! Don't make me hurt you!'' She tossed out the last remark as a kind of skewed, ironic jest—hoping to make him believe she was unmoved. When she heard it with her own ears, she held out no hope that he would accept it to be anything but the pathetic farce it was.

"How much more hurt can I take?'' he asked, his voice cracking with emotion.

Movement caught Susan's eye and she realized one of the flight attendants had come out of her momentary stupor. "Excuse me, sir?'' She touched Jake's shoulder. "You'll have to take a seat.''

He paid the attendant no heed, and continued to watch Susan's face. "I'm not flying to California, darling.'' He took her hand in both of his. "I'm staying, and so are you.''

"No,'' she murmured, a tear spilling down her cheek. She realized now she had been wrong to run away. She'd been a selfish coward. She should have stayed, told him the truth, no matter how painful. This humiliating spectacle was a thousand times worse—for both of them. Blinking back tears so that she could see him clearly, she said the words she'd dreaded even to think. "I—I can't give you want you want, Jake. I can't—''

"I want you! Just you.'' He brushed a kiss across her trembling lips. "We can adopt, darling. Please, don't leave me.''

His lips brushed hers again as he murmured, "Stay.''

He sat back on his heels, his expression so galvanizing it took away her ability to breathe. She felt dizzy, unsure. "What did you say?'' she asked weakly.

A rueful smile lifted the corners of his mouth. "I said, we can adopt.''

"Adopt?"

He nodded, the tenderness in his eyes stunning her.

"You know?" she whispered, not daring to believe it.

"I know." He brushed away a tear, and kissed the place beneath her eye where it had been. "Please come home with me."

Suddenly, like a dam bursting, her heart overflowed with joy. She felt insubstantial and light-headed, but deliriously happy. "I—I love you so much, Jake." She smiled faintly, wanting to hug him, but she couldn't seem to lift her arms. Clearly this whole unbelievable experience had somehow shorted out a part of her brain. "But—I—I can't seem to move."

With a hearty laugh, he flipped open her seatbelt and lifted her into his arms. "Darling, I can take care of that." His smile took on a charming boldness. "Do you think you'll be up to a moonlight picnic, Mrs. Merit?" he whispered, his tone delightfully provocative.

She slipped her arms around his neck and kissed his jaw. "I'll clear my calendar." Her soft teasing stoked the gentle fire of passion in his eyes. For the first time in her life, she felt utterly contented, whole, and loved.

Snuggling in the harbor of Jake's arms, Susan was swept from the plane by her big, strong husband, just ahead of the closing door.

When Susan and Jake returned to Merit Island, their lives took a decided turn for the better. At last, Jake found what had been missing in his life. His marvelous, indispensable Susan—who courageously and without fanfare, rescued the heart he thought he'd lost forever.

And being a devoted, considerate husband, he promptly gave it back to her—for safekeeping.

* * * * *

Coming Soon

Marc Merit, big city doctor, yearned for a simpler life, and returned home to Merit Island, ready to settle down and start a family. The last thing he expected to find was Mimi Baptiste, a free spirit who called the world her home and knew there was never enough time to see it all.
A country doctor's days and nights are never his own, an entangled existence Mimi wanted no part of. And the pretty, strong-willed wayfarer was the last woman on earth Marc should be attracted to. He knew her driving passion in life was to find out what was beyond the next hill, and the next and the next...
Watch Marc and Mimi battle the attraction as their destinies collide in *COMING HOME TO WED*
Renee Roszel's next novel in her
THE MERITS OF MARRIAGE miniseries.

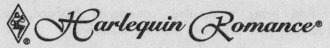